# ACTIVITY PAGE:

Cut the hole out of the front cover to help Carrie find her friends!

PRAISE FOR

# SEX CHANGE AND THE CITY

"*Sex Change and the City* awoke something within me . . . not gender stuff but a deep, dark desire to actually watch all of *Sex and the City* (arguably a much more impressive task). Maybe it just speaks to the fact that all the coolest, cleverest queers contributing to *SCATC* make the show seem actually appealing. I laughed, I cried, I got a little horny about Charlotte getting force-masced. 10/10, thank you Girl Dad Press!"

**—KENDRA WELLS, author of *Real Hero Shit***

"A sharp, hysterical collection for everyone who loves the you you love. If our ladies read this for a book club, Charlotte would arrive with a list of 40 discussion points, Samantha would have a story for all of them, Miranda's copy would be dogeared and littered in underlines, and Carrie wouldn't finish it. And that's just fabulous."

**—BOBBY FINGER, host of *Who? Weekly* and author of *Four Squares***

"A text as rich and varied and messy as the show itself. I loved it even though I got stuck with only 2 shoes in the MASH game!"

**—KELSEY MCKINNEY, founding host of *Normal Gossip* and author of *You Didn't Hear This From Me***

"*Sex Change in the City* is the funny, loveable, outsider book I've been missing; filled with writers clearly having a good time using the premise to lay out real truths. It achieves the rare art of the best humor: a joke that tells you something dead serious about life."

**—TORREY PETERS, author of *Detransition, Baby***

"Fran Lebowitz (*SATC* S4E2) once observed that the AIDS epidemic killed more than a generation of artists; it killed the greatest, most discerning audience members of all time. *Sex Change and the City* is a celebration of queer discernment, fandom, and cultural consumption. Every page of this book is a good time, especially the trans Steve erotica."

**—MADDY COURT, author of *The Ex-Girlfriend of My Ex-Girlfriend Is My Girlfriend***

"Harron Walker, Dani Janae, Mattie Lubchansky, Fancy Feast, Juno Carmel and dozens more queer and trans artists going long on the aspects of the *Sex and the City* extended universe that they can't stop thinking about? It's giving fever dream—and it's also giving perfect, perfect book. If you've always longed for the experience of watching *SATC* with your funniest, smartest, most depraved friends (or just always wondered what would happen if Aidan and Steve happened to fuck) you need to buy a copy this very minute."

**—EMMA SPECTER, *Vogue* culture writer and author of *More, Please***

"When did everybody stop smoking? When did everybody pair off? Girl Dad Press used to be the most exciting publisher in the world. Now it's nothing but smoking near a fucking open window. Anthologies are so over. O.V.E.R. Over! No one's fun anymore. Whatever happened to fun! God. I'm so bored I could die. Splat!"

**—SABRINA IMBLER, author of *How Far the Light Reaches***

# SEX CHANGE AND THE CITY

EDITED BY
TUCK WOODSTOCK
& NIKO STRATIS

SEX CHANGE AND THE CITY


Candace Bushnell initially launched *Sex and the City* as a newspaper column in *The New York Observer* in 1994. Darren Star's *Sex and the City* TV show was created in 1998 for HBO. In 2021, Michael Patrick King revived the series with *And Just Like That . . .* on HBO Max. We thank all of these creators and their legal teams for being chill about our little book.

Cover illustration by Mattie Lubchansky
Interior design by Jakob Vala
Edited by Tuck Woodstock & Niko Stratis

Published by Girl Dad Press
Printed by Radix Printing & Publishing Cooperative in Brooklyn, NY
First edition, November 2025

ISBN: 979-8-9997158-0-7

*for Karen Covergirl*

"I don't want to be in a situation for even an hour where I'm not enjoying myself."

—Kim Cattrall

# Contents

## TUCK WOODSTOCK

# Introduction

## Welcome to the Straight People Zoo

A military-themed barbecue restaurant; a bridal shower on Long Island; a college football tailgate at a Wisconsin fraternity; a John Mayer concert in 2006. At some point, despite our best efforts, we have all found ourselves visiting some version of what I call the Straight People Zoo.[1]

These zones of peak heterosexuality are fascinating up to a point, with their cryptic social customs and bizarre mating rituals. But despite my perverse fascination with the intricacies of straight culture, I prefer to engage at a safe distance, in a venue with quick and accessible exits. So while you won't spot me on safari at the country music festival in Tampa or the Fourth of July car show in Reno, you just might find me visiting my favorite virtual Straight People Zoo—that is to say, watching *Sex and the City*.

---

1. That military barbecue spot is a national chain, by the way. They opened their first location on 9/11/11 *on purpose*, and every day at noon, they play the national anthem and encourage their customers to stand. Help!

My SPZ excursions to *SATC* have taught me so much. For example, I've learned that straight people will lust after a white jazz bassist in a porkpie hat, but flee when they suspect he has ADHD (S4E4).[2] They do not get tested for STIs; they do not even necessarily know what chlamydia *is* (S3E6). If pressured, they will abandon their favorite vibrator (S1E9) or dump a guy for eating pussy *too well* (S2E3). This is why I love the Straight People Zoo: for all the hardships that queer people face (structural oppression, polycule drama, etc.), it's reassuring to remember that the alternatives are somehow worse.[3]

It is in this spirit—celebrating queer cultural superiority in the face of whatever heterosexuals are doing—that I first conceptualized *Sex Change and the City*. But while my approach was anthropological at best (and gawking at worst), many submissions surprised me by earnestly empathizing with the characters of *SATC*. Despite artist Sarah Esocoff's claim that *everyone* is a Miranda because "she's the only one who isn't completely ridiculous,"[4] our contributors connected

---

2. Can you imagine trying to date queer people while avoiding neurodivergence? There simply wouldn't be anyone left to date.

3. As a journalist, I can acknowledge that *Sex and the City* should not serve as my single definitive source for straight culture. Not only are these women all white, wealthy Manhattanites, but they are also, crucially, fictional characters whose words were often written by gay guys. For this reason, I have visited other virtual SPZs, such as *Married at First Sight* and various *Real Housewives*, and while I cannot confirm any specifics, I feel confident in my general conclusion that It's Bad Out There.

4. Esocoff, Sarah. "Quiz. Which '*Sex and the City*' Character Are You? And Don't Lie, We'll Know." *Points in Case*, 12 Jan. 2021, www.pointsincase.com/articles/quiz-which-sex-and-the-city-character-are-you

with Charlotte's repressed curiosity, Carrie's cringeworthy romanticism, and Samantha's stubborn independence. Their work explores the shame of secret relationships, the rage of middle age, the grief of losing a parent . . . and, of course, the embarrassment of being nonbinary.[5]

Perhaps this all sounds heavy for a book titled *Sex Change and the City*. If so, let me assure you that, much like its source material, this anthology rarely remains serious for more than five consecutive minutes. Between essays on rejection and regret, readers can expect plenty of Sex (mostly featuring Steve with various genitalia) and the City (via a guided bus tour across Manhattan), as well as comics, paintings, poetry, Mad Libs, M.A.S.H., and a roleplaying game. Immediately after one of *SCATC*'s most emotionally devastating pieces, you will find a literal picture of an ass.

We've curated the book this way because we assume you've come to the Straight People Zoo in the hope of having fun. To that end, we don't devote many pages to litigating *Sex and the City*'s countless sins. Rather than sternly condemning Samantha for mistreating her trans neighbors, we subject her to the Ghosts of Transexual Past, Present, and Future. Instead of explaining why biphobia is bad, we contrast Carrie's visit to "Alice In Confused-Sexual-Orientation Land" with a bisexual writer's experience at their first straight party (on a Williamsburg rooftop, natch). We don't dissect *SCATC*'s countless instances of racism, not because the show isn't *so very deeply* racist, but because we assume you've already suffered through those episodes and might instead enjoy learning which *SATC*

5. I regret to say that, yes, we legally *must* acknowledge Che and Rock at some point.

quote is your breakup style or which of Carrie's companions is most likely to start HRT.[6]

I do sometimes wonder whether it's imprudent to expend resources on another goofy anthology when everyone is, you know, suffering. In the months since we announced this project, the United States government has upheld healthcare bans for trans youth, restricted trans passport access, and abducted thousands of immigrants. One could certainly argue that our collective time would be better spent compounding our own estrogen, hosting Know Your Rights workshops, or rebuilding the orchiectomy barn.[7] (See you there, Steve!) But perhaps we don't need to choose; we can organize mutual aid networks *and* share weird, hot, silly, queer art. If nothing else, this collection is a reminder that although our adversaries might attempt to ban our books and erase us from the public record, they ultimately cannot prevent us from publishing whatever we want—whether it's meditations on trans phenomenology or something called "Mr. Big's Phalloplasty Emporium."

---

6. To recap: despite Manhattan's majority-minority population, the original series depicts the borough as eerily white. In addition, several *SATC* plotlines are egregiously racist; examples include Samantha's storylines in "The Caste System" (S2E10), "No Ifs, Ands or Butts" (S3E5), and the movie *Sex and the City 2*. For a firsthand perspective, I recommend *Vanity Fair*'s interview with Sundra Oakley, the actor who played Adeena in "No Ifs, Ands or Butts." (Desta, Yohana. "Being One of the Only Black Actresses on *Sex and the City* Was a 'Surreal' Experience." *Vanity Fair*, 8 June 2018, www.vanityfair.com/hollywood/2018/06/sex-and-the-city-sundra-oakley)

7. Dodds, Io. "'Never ask permission': How two trans women ran a legendary underground surgical clinic in a rural tractor barn" *The Independent*, 3 July 2022, www.independent.co.uk/news/world/americas/trans-history-underground-sugical-clinic-b2114777.html

As you make your way through this collection, I hope it brings you the same comfort as your favorite episode of *Sex and the City*.[8] Believe it or not, you are not the first person to ever struggle at work, or date someone terrible, or be rejected by a cool, artsy dyke. And hey, maybe you can't stop hooking up with [insert your least favorite astrological sign here], but at least you are hot and gay and have never been dumped via Post-it note! It could really be so much worse.[9]

That's the joy of the Straight People Zoo, of course; so often, trans and queer people are seen as oddities to be poked, prodded, and locked away. But we have escaped our enclosures! We are running amok! We are writing Aidan/Steve slashfic and drawing the *Sex and the City* cast as puppy girls! And just like that, here we are: thriving on the other side of the glass.

---

8. Or, if you're a *SATC* hater, I hope this book affirms your existing opinions / critiques / hot takes / etc.

9. I'm assuming that, if you're reading this, you are hot and gay . . . or at least hot and bisexual.

# sex change and the city

# Shot Day

We asked our contributors which *Sex and the City* character would be most likely to start HRT.

**Miranda Hobbes (7 votes)**

*See "Help! My Miranda Is A Man! (Duh!)" on pg. 92.*

**Charlotte York (6 votes)**

*See "Total Charlotte" on pg. 78.*

**Samantha Jones (5 votes)**

"I subscribe to Alex V. Green's theory that Samantha is a stealth transexual woman. That said, if Samantha wasn't a transexual woman, I would say she'd go on testosterone for the clitoral growth, then realize she's a gay guy"—Diana

"Samantha has tried both T and E recreationally" —Flórián

"Samantha is canonically on HRT in *SATC2*"—Mattie

**Steve Brady (3 votes)**

*See "Shooting Hoops With My Buddy Steve" on pg. 152.*

**Skipper Johnston (3 votes)**

"Do we really think women keep breaking up with Skipper Johnston because he's a "nice guy"? Instead of chasing women who want bad things, maybe Skipper should try becoming one"—Jas Brown

**Trey MacDougal (3 votes)**

"I like to think that a lot of his mommy issues and sexual hang-ups would untangle if he allowed himself to become the beautiful Scottish lady he was always meant to be. He'd also probably become more invested in how he decorated his space and the general trajectory of his life"—Jesse

**Jack Berger (2 votes)**

"'I think my discomfort with your public recognition and my own obsession with traditional emblems of masculinity like this motorcycle are symptoms of my own dysphoria, so I have to break up with you. I love you AND I want to be you' is kind of too long to fit on a Post-it note, no?"—Bri

**Aidan Shaw (2 votes)**

"Aidan would be a stunning woman and would absolutely sweep NYC's lesbian community as a sexy trans woodworker"—Juno

### Mr. Big (2 votes)

"I have a sense that Mr. Big employs a lot of gender-affirming care in his later years"—Chae

"Mr. Big is an egg for shuuuuure"—A.M.

### Harry Goldenblatt (2 votes)

"She wants to be beautiful like Charlotte, and Charlotte and the kids support her"—Rowan

### Laney Berlin (2 votes)

"Laney is always getting drunk and yelling, 'Who wants to see my tits?' Looking for any reason to go shirtless is trans masc behaviour. Also, imagine this bit post-top surgery and it's just Laney showing off their top surgery scars as people cheer? ALSO, you do you Laney but a name suggestion: Lane Berlin is giving some real Fred Astaire dapper retro Hollywood leading man energy"—Quinn K.

"Testosterone could have saved him. . . . . . ." —Harron

### Smith Jerrod (1 vote)

"She realizes that she was only able to keep up with Samantha for so long because she wanted to be her" —Daniel

### Enid Frick (1 vote)

"She would do a really fab HRT commercial a la Patti LaBelle"—Alex

**Vaughn Wysel (1 vote)**

"[My guess is] Justin Theroux when he played that author whose mom had a really nice brownstone and served bagels & lox"—Georgia

**Carrie Bradshaw (0 votes)**

She'd never go for it. But would it fix her? Funny you should ask . . .

OZZY LLINAS GOODMAN

# Carrie Bradshaw, Transition Already!

I have a strong memory of browsing the dollar section at a Bookstar around 2004 and picking up a copy of some Fox News pundit's book about feminism.[1] As a sheltered but curious queer child, I naturally seized the chance to flip to the chapter about sex. What I found, strangely enough, was an essay arguing that *Sex and the City*, far from portraying liberated women's sex lives, was clearly about the sex lives of gay men. Yes, the contemporary conservative case against *Sex and the City* was that it was *transsexual*—portraying straight women doing things that only gay men are supposed to do.

I'm sure this stuck with me all these years for no particular reason. But I always assumed that Fox News lady was just sort of talking out of her ass. Imagine my surprise when, a decade or so later, I finally got around to watching the show. In the very first episode, narrator Carrie Bradshaw decides to try

1. Thanks to Daniel Lanza Rivers' essay on pg. 160, I recently realized that this was Ann Coulter's book *How to Talk to a Liberal (If You Must)*, which is not strictly about feminism, but whatever.

having sex "like a man." (Translation: She won't bottom, and she will leave immediately after she comes—and before he does.) Carrie has a great time, but tragically, she decides never to repeat the experience. Her main goal was to get revenge on a fuckboy from her past, and it seems he didn't mind this brush with homosexuality. Carrie moves on when it becomes clear her gender transgression isn't hurting her ex in the way she wanted.

I'm reminded of the number of advice questions we receive over at *Gender Reveal* that are some version of "How can I make everyone around me react perfectly to my transition?" Carrie needs to hear the answer too: Even if you do your best impression of "man," it's possible your sex partners won't react in the ways you want them to. You can obsess, or you can move on and maybe try different sex partners! Unfortunately, despite her investment in the trans art of fucking around and finding out, Carrie isn't exactly on a queer mission of self-discovery. She's too invested in figuring out the desires of the men she dates to spend much time considering her own. Never mind the fact that she doesn't seem to even like the majority of these men! She understands that in order to date the kind of wealthy white man she aspires to marry, she must be the kind of woman such a man wants.

It is *very* trans to be trying so hard to do a gender that doesn't really seem to be making you happy. Carrie's attempts to diagnose and catalog the dating norms of elite New Yorkers remind me of my own pre-transition attempts to understand cishet dating norms: hopeless, joyless, and doomed to failure. Somehow, Carrie never seems to internalize the fact that she's having a bad time overall, maybe because she's so distracted by other people's opinions. Like in S1E3, "Bay of Married

Pigs," when a close friend's husband flashes his dick at Carrie. She freaks out about this, but not because of the actual incident—it's because her married friends are now shunning her for being an unwed, irresistible mantrap. Carrie is thrilled when her friend "forgives" her, rather than questioning what kind of friends would treat her this way in the first place.

The show presents marriage-obsessed Charlotte as the prude, but all four main characters have pretty boring views of sex.[2] (Carrie might actually be the most sexually conservative—she's certainly the one who has spent the least time as a lesbian!) Queer characters are present for punchlines, for subplots, and for a fun party, but they rarely take center stage. In fact, the girls are *so* straight that, at times, they seem to de-gay the people around them. In S2E2, "The Awful Truth," after Charlotte expresses her hesitation to try anal, Carrie's gay best friend Stanford quips, "Personally, I don't like anything in my ass, and I know that may come as a surprise." Given the number of gay men involved in the writing and production of the show, it's hard to read this moment as anything other than pandering to straight audiences.[3] (Stanford, baby, WHY!)

Fundamentally, *Sex and the City* is about the fact that the sex you're having can only be fully understood in the context

---

2. Samantha's approach is the most pleasure-focused, which I think makes it the queerest. But I also find it tiresome how many of her relationship problems stem from the configuration and functioning of her partners' genitals. It's not that such things are never relevant, but surely if nothing else, queerness is about sex not having to be defined by what's between our legs.

3. Ed. note: The only other explanation we could think of is that Darren Star et al. are devout sides.

of your sexual community. In the case of Carrie, Miranda, Charlotte, and Samantha, that community is overwhelmingly straight. The queer people involved seem to get some sort of straight contact high, becoming ever more obsessed with monogamy and marriage the more time they spend around Carrie and her friends. Still, as Carrie fights for a semi-traditional heterosexuality, she manages to make a lot of other kinds of sex look hotter and more fun. This is especially true in S2E3, "The Freak Show," in which the friends pressure Charlotte into dumping a man who gives her seven orgasms in a row because of his "freakish" obsession with oral sex. If there's a message here, it's clearly about the dangers of investing too deeply in normality at the expense of what you really enjoy.

At times, it seems like Carrie realizes this, and is on the brink of rejecting a traditional heterosexual narrative. She struggles with monogamy throughout the series, and in the season 2 finale, she considers that maybe she wasn't meant to be married, comparing herself to a wild horse who can't be tamed. In season 4, she learns sex tips from gay porn and breaks out in hives at the idea of getting straight-married. But the end of the series sees her determine that the problem wasn't monogamous heterosexuality—she just had the wrong guy!

Even if Carrie Bradshaw will never transition, I think she might be doing some sort of mutual aid work in documenting the cishet community. Consider S1E8, "Three's A Crowd," in which Miranda learns the age-old lesson that unicorn hunters exist and are, unfortunately, generally too off-putting to have sex with. Or S2E6, "The Cheating Curve," in which Samantha discovers the joys of erotic shaving. Alan Cumming plays a nonbinary(?) stylist who changes their name to

O. Samantha stands to pee at the gay club. Charlotte gets seduced by a chaser who force-mascs her. When the show is at its most queer, it's also at its most entertaining. It's too bad the characters themselves don't seem to see it. Carrie, you know where to find us if you change your mind!

JESSE ROBKIN

# Secret Sex and the Self

"She's not someone I date openly." I'm sure I'm not the only trans woman whose body tenses at this line with visceral familiarity.

In the season 1 episode "Secret Sex," Carrie stumbles across her friend Mike at Fenghua, a clandestine Szechuan spot. Mike is with a woman named Libby, though we only learn her name because Carrie makes a point to introduce herself; Mike doesn't assist with the introduction at all. The next day, Carrie grills Mike on what happened. Is Libby married? Is she a cousin? Mike says no. He tells Carrie that Libby is "smart, incredibly sweet, and the sex is great." So why hide the relationship? It sounds like Mike found a total catch.

"She's just not the one I see myself with," Mike explains. He doesn't consider Libby "that gorgeous," and he seems rather put off by her cheesemonger profession. Despite their proven compatibility, Mike thinks she's not the right woman for him "in the larger sense." In other words, Libby has fallen short of Mike's Platonic ideal of a significant other—an ideal she certainly never asked to compete against.

This kind of evaluation is all too common, especially within the straight dating scene. Though it's by no means unique to a single gender, many cishet men in particular carry in their heads a hazy image of their hypothetical future wife. Every lover is measured against this image and, if she's found wanting, relegated to the status of "discreet hookup" or "short-term relationship." For trans women, this verdict is even more likely, as the mere fact of our transness sometimes overshadows all our other desirable traits. Before I fully understood this, I often found myself running up against a wall between my relationship and my lover's life outside the relationship—indeed, outside the bedroom.

This is why my body remembers Libby's plight: I've lived it. Given Mike's perception of her worth, Libby's job as a cheesemonger might as well be an imperceptible Y chromosome within her DNA. Mike asks Carrie to keep the relationship a secret. Naturally, she puts it in her column.

"How many of us are having great sex with people we're ashamed to introduce to our friends?" Carrie writes. She doesn't ask, "How many of us are having great sex with people who are ashamed to introduce us to their friends?" Watching Carrie unpack the implications of Mike's behavior with her readers, I found myself wondering why this was even Mike's story in the first place. Why is Carrie so much more invested in the psychology behind Mike's secrecy than she is in how Libby feels about it? It's as if Carrie feels more affinity for Mike than she does for Libby, despite later wondering if she is Mr. Big's Libby. What's more, by not talking to Libby or even attempting to see things from her point of view, Carrie has effectively validated Mike's devaluation. Libby has no agency here, either within her relationship with Mike or in how Carrie frames the relationship to her readers.

I relate to Libby, so I have a pretty good idea of how she feels. This might be something that has happened to her before. When she started recognizing signs of Mike's embarrassment, she may have thought, "Oh God, not again." She had been vulnerable with Mike; did that make his betrayal all the more hurtful? Will this make her less inclined to offer that same vulnerability to future partners? Does she agree with Mike's assessment of her worth? It's hard to tell, since Carrie doesn't get her side of the story, but certainly at Fenghua, Libby doesn't attempt to take introductions into her own hands. It's as if she implicitly knows that doing so would not be acceptable behavior within the relationship.

I get it, girl. My lovers who wouldn't claim me in public taught me, too, that I was not a person to be claimed. When I reentered the dating pool a year or two into my transition, I encountered a string of cis people, men and women, who would express private desire for me but rarely public. The first was a cis woman I dated for nearly a year. Among the myriad problems in our relationship was my feeling invisible to most of her social and professional life. Since the breakup, I have more than once told a mutual acquaintance that I dated her, only for them to look at me shocked and say, "I didn't know she was queer!"

A short while later, I found myself in a six-month situationship with a cis man I'd met through a shared hobby. Our secret sex before or after meeting up with our friend group was hot at first, but ultimately contributed to my increasingly negative self-perception. Once I recognized this pattern, I grew emotionally calloused, reluctant to fully give myself to future partners. I rarely pursued anyone in whom I felt strong interest for fear of what they might privately think of me. Instead, I almost exclusively dated people who approached me first, for whom I felt very little. Ironically, this adopted aloofness probably turned me into a Mike, as I became the one uncomfortable claiming these relationships with my friends.

Did this create a cycle, whereby the people I treated this way went on to do the same to others? I don't know. It does seem like a risk, though, with this kind of treatment; when we show our partners they are not worthy of our love, they may go on to find partners about whom they feel the same.

In Libby's case, it seems she may have broken free from any potential behavioral cycle. Though in the restaurant she doesn't stick up for herself, by the end of "Secret Sex," she has found a new lover who isn't ashamed of her. As for me, it took longer than a 30-minute episode, but I have also unlearned much of the shame I once felt about myself. I'm of course not immune to poor treatment, but when I do encounter it, I'm now much better equipped to recognize it as a "them" problem, not a "me" problem.

Perhaps this is the true lesson from "Secret Sex." Mike eventually underwent the internal work necessary to go public with his love for Libby, but in that time, Libby also did the necessary work to love herself. Mike lost out on an interesting, ultimately self-assured woman—and a potential lifetime of exotic cheese—all because he was not self-assured enough himself to believe his friends would value him regardless of who he dated. The longer we neglect our own self-worth, the more damage we do to the people who try to love us, and the more likely we are to lose our brief chance to love them back.

DREW THELKE

# The Cast of *Sex and the City* As Puppy Girls . . .

# . . . Except for Samantha Who Is a Cat Of Course

# MY LAPTOP, MY MOM

Season 4, episode 8 of *Sex and the City* is called "My Motherboard, My Self," but whenever I look it up I search *Miranda's mom dies*. I type it as if it's a warning, and as the girls chat in Bryant Park at the episode's opening, I want to warn Miranda, myself. *Miranda, mom dies*. Moms die, and my mom died on December 11, 2022 (and every day after that). Miranda's mom dies over and over again on my TV.

Frustratingly, the main plot of the episode is about Carrie's laptop crashing. Aidan tries a Windows shortcut on the Mac device. The Tekserve guy says, "You're not compatible," and Carrie predictably spirals. I struggle to be generous with Carrie as she continues to call back to her stupid computer after Miranda's mom dies. When Miranda calls to tell Carrie that her mother passed away overnight, alone, she says, "They called and said she was crashing," a reminder that this story isn't about Miranda or her mother, but Carrie's laptop.

Carrie says, "I'm sure on some level she knew you were with her." Miranda says, "But I wasn't with her. Nobody was."

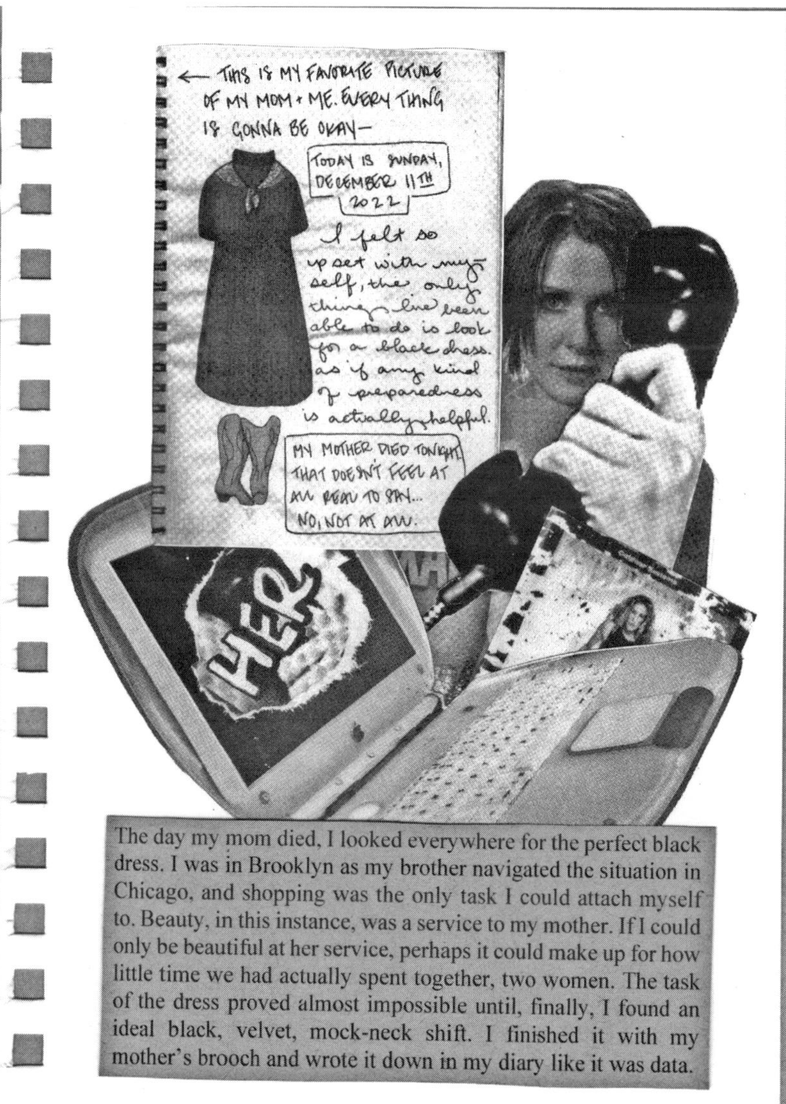


The day my mom died, I looked everywhere for the perfect black dress. I was in Brooklyn as my brother navigated the situation in Chicago, and shopping was the only task I could attach myself to. Beauty, in this instance, was a service to my mother. If I could only be beautiful at her service, perhaps it could make up for how little time we had actually spent together, two women. The task of the dress proved almost impossible until, finally, I found an ideal black, velvet, mock-neck shift. I finished it with my mother's brooch and wrote it down in my diary like it was data.

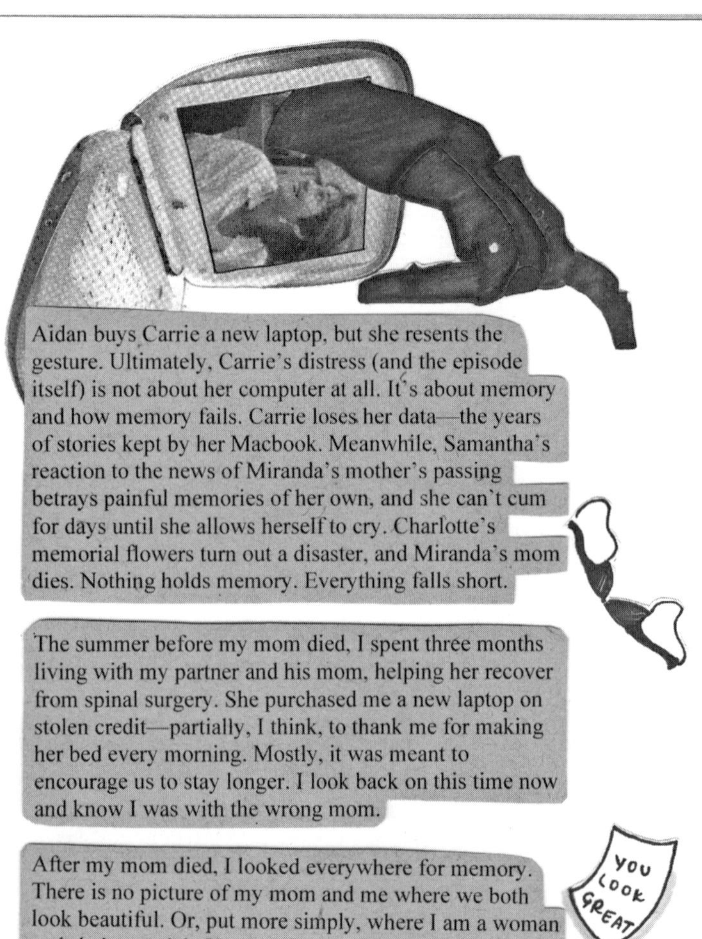


Aidan buys Carrie a new laptop, but she resents the gesture. Ultimately, Carrie's distress (and the episode itself) is not about her computer at all. It's about memory and how memory fails. Carrie loses her data—the years of stories kept by her Macbook. Meanwhile, Samantha's reaction to the news of Miranda's mother's passing betrays painful memories of her own, and she can't cum for days until she allows herself to cry. Charlotte's memorial flowers turn out a disaster, and Miranda's mom dies. Nothing holds memory. Everything falls short.

The summer before my mom died, I spent three months living with my partner and his mom, helping her recover from spinal surgery. She purchased me a new laptop on stolen credit—partially, I think, to thank me for making her bed every morning. Mostly, it was meant to encourage us to stay longer. I look back on this time now and know I was with the wrong mom.

After my mom died, I looked everywhere for memory. There is no picture of my mom and me where we both look beautiful. Or, put more simply, where I am a woman and she's not sick. Her smell fades from every blanket, and I cannot draw her. I can only draw myself. Miranda wears a knee-length black dress with matching jacket to her mother's service, along with what I'd like to think is her mom's brooch.

I never knew this but, at some point toward the end of her life, my mom made a second Facebook. She had requested me, but I thought it was a bot and never asked her about it. The week after she passed, I accepted the request and was heartsick to find how much I had missed. Heartsick and lifted – suddenly there was more of her to discover. I spend so much time on my mom's two Facebook pages. I check them every day.

I want to tell Miranda that her mom dies. I want to tell her that they won't be together, and that there won't be last words. I want to tell her that at the moment the veil is lifted, her psychic mother will have no one to tell what she sees. Not at that moment, anyway.

I want to tell Miranda the black dress helps and the new bra helps, too. The brooch helps. For now, my memories are stored in the laptop and that helps as much as anything else. It all falls short and it all helps the same amount.

CONNER REED

# A Letter from Pedro Almodóvar to Michael Patrick King

Dear Michael Patrick King,

Heyy diva. I'm taking a break from shooting that gay cowboy thing with Pedro Pascal and Ethan Hawke so I can write this down before I forget. Basically, I think your show is so awesome. *Sex and the City.* I'd been meaning to check it out ever since Penelope Cruz told me how much fun she had performing as "the senior vice president of the Bank of Madrid" for 30 seconds in *Sex and the City 2.* She never did get to see the rest of that film, but we've had many discussions about how culturally sensitive we assume it must be!

Earlier this week, I finally decided to take the plunge. After a long day of coaching Ethan and Pedro through the ins and outs of homoerotic gunplay, I kicked back, poured myself a glass of Barfutura's weird wine that is based on my effete photography, and started from the top. (For me, the "top" of any television program is season 4, episode 4.) Imagine my surprise when, moments after the woman in the tutu saw herself on the bus advertisement, I discovered that you'd created not a frivolous peak-empire fairytale but a glorious story of love between women!

From the moment the libidinous blonde friend tells the rest of her cohort that she is "having a relationship" with the passionate gallerist Maria, my heart stopped. Here it was. My white whale. My *Moby-Dyke*. In my films, I have covered a lot of ground: obsession, sexual violence, forced feminization, the way the far-reaching psychological reverberations of Spanish fascism can cause women to steal babies and fuck their mothers. The only thing I haven't covered? Real sapphic love. Which is painful, because I love women. I love it when they wear jewelry, when they cry, when they teeter precariously on the precipice of a nervous breakdown. Many in the Spanish press have argued for decades that my oeuvre reeks of misogyny, but I ask you this, Michael: would a gay guy who hates women make so many movies where they live in amazing apartments?

All to say, I'm writing to you with a proposal. Given what I can only assume was a rapturous response to *Sex and the City 2*, I'd like to direct another film in the franchise that more deeply explores the relationship between your divine blonde floozy and her lesbian lover. My film would, of course, maintain the tone of the original series: elegiac, mournful, politically potent. Perhaps the blonde friend could be played by Ana de Armas, so brilliant as Marilyn Monroe in Andrew Dominik's fiercely feminist fable a few years back. (I believe the original blonde left the franchise to play the upright bass full-time.) Perhaps Maria could be played by Penelope Cruz with hair extensions.

If you're reluctant to give up rights to the material, I understand. I can only hope that my writing convinces you that I see the dramatic potential here. For an episode of TV that must have aired sometime between 1974 and 1977, given the limited sexual vocabulary, you and your team achieved a remarkably forward-thinking air of personal liberation. After Ana de Armas (you'll forgive me if I have made the characters my own in recent days) lets her friends know she is gay now, the group walks home in a daze. "How does that work?" asks the intrepid Carrie Bradshaw in her Cool Britannia beret. "You go to bed one night, you wake up the next morning, and poof, you're a lesbian?"

Such stabs at empathy moved me. Here is a woman who has plastered her face on buses all across New York City, careening through the streets of Chelsea as an unholy human-automotive hybrid, but who cannot quite imagine herself capable of true transformation. "I'm a shoe. I always wanted to be one, and poof, now I am," she jokes to her friends, trying in vain to grasp at Ana de Armas's effortless rejection of stable identity markers. Then she's off to get eaten out by a jazz musician with murder in his eyes. The tragedy of heterosexuality, the ennui of the dominant class: it's all there. Now imagine if everyone was wearing so much fucking eyeshadow, forming tableaus that nod to the compositions of Edward Hopper, and constantly under threat of breaking into song. (Once, while we were doing lines in Venice, Leos Carax told me he could help me book Kylie Minogue for a musical number. Just an idea!)

I don't want to appear too eager, and I've finished my weird wine, so I'll leave my request there. Please think it over and get back to me at your earliest convenience. A twink assistant of mine has let me know that you are hard at work on the third season of something he called "the agony and ecstasy of Che Diaz," which is no problem at all. Sounds like my kind of melodrama.

In any event, I look forward to watching a second episode of *Sex and the City* soon!

Yours,
Pedro Almodóvar

P.S. If you're wondering why I decided to write you this letter in English, it's because I'm preparing to write my extremely normal script for *The Room Next Door* in English, too. It is set to star Tilda Swinton and Julianne Moore, but they don't kiss in it, so don't even ask.

BRI LEROSE

# Not Well, Bitch:

## *SATC*, the *Real Housewives*, and the Rage of Middle Age

I invented a fun new party game to play with gay people called Sex-or-RHONY. All you have to do is list plot details from *Sex and the City* or its reality counterpart, *The Real Housewives of New York*, and have players guess which show you're describing.

Here, it's easy: Somebody throws their prosthetic leg on the dinner table. *RHONY*! A coked-up old party girl falls out of a window. *SATC*! Two estranged best friends squash a decade-old beef at one of their husband's funerals. Uhh . . . *Both!* Come to think of it, maybe it's not so easy to tell truth from fiction when it comes to the messy, middle-aged women of New York.

The two franchises have intersected many times throughout their respective runs. Bravo boss Andy Cohen has had two cameos on *Sex and the City* (one as a Barney's shoe salesman, naturally). Candace Bushnell, author of the original *SATC* columns in the *New York Observer*, has been friends with the women of *RHONY* for more than 30 years—in fact, she has appeared on several episodes of *Housewives* as a bemused dinner party guest. Rumor has it Bushnell was even being considered to officially join the cast of *Housewives* at one point, before the show got rebooted and tossed out all of the beloved, tight-knit sixty-somethings who'd been drinking and fucking and fighting on Bravo for over a decade, in favor of a younger, blander cast of characters who barely knew each other. The Seema Patel Effect.[1]

But a different connection between two of the series' characters gives us a valuable insight into something unexpected: the rage of middle age. Through these women, the shows examine, intentionally or otherwise, the pent-up anger of decades that didn't turn out as you planned, and what it does to the people around you. Whether you are the perpetrator, the recipient, or simply a witness to this existential rage of a life that's been harsher than promised, you are not getting out of here unscathed.

The two characters in question are *SATC*'s Susan Sharon, a martini-drinking Italian cashmere importer and friend of Carrie's, and *RHONY*'s Dorinda Medley, a martini-drinking Italian cashmere importer on whom the character of Susan Sharon was allegedly based (although Candace Bushnell has publicly denied the connection). Both women's "storylines" often revolve around their husbands—Sharon's is an angry man named Richard who's constantly yelling at her, and Medley's is the deceased love of her life (also named Richard), whose sudden loss rendered Dorinda a vicious loose cannon.

---

1. Why, yes, I did have to look up this character's name just now! You ever blow off your lifelong group of girlfriends in favor of your real estate agent because you both love smoking cigs?

Candace Bushnell happens to be on the receiving end of a famous Dorinda explosion and one of *RHONY*'s most iconic lines of all time. In S9E4, "The Etiquette of Friendship," Bushnell and Medley are just two of a table full of blonde-haired women in black sweaters at a Hamptons dinner party. Dorinda comes in hot, already full of barely-concealed rage due to something castmate Sonja Morgan allegedly leaked to the press. As it often does, Dorinda's rage spills out quickly and publicly, and she immediately aims below the belt. Midway through a verbal tirade at Morgan, Dorinda fires off, unprompted, "Why don't you stop getting vaginal rejuvenation and put an EZ Pass on that vagina with your Holland Tunnel." Dorinda continues to unload every round of ammunition she has, leaving the other guests shifting uncomfortably. Later, Dorinda turns to Candace Bushnell and recaps her outburst with an incredible one-liner, since meme'd into oblivion: "How am I doing? *Not well, bitch.*" In a talking head interview that follows, a battered Sonja says simply: "That's just not how one acts normally at a dinner party." This all happens 18 minutes into the episode. It is incredible television.

What's interesting about this moment, beyond Dorinda's legendary quotability, is the way the other women respond to her vitriol. Each cast member seems to default to different survival instincts: Countess Luann piles onto Sonja. Carole Radziwill shrugs, as if to say, "Sonja had it coming." And Candace Bushnell herself is simply a witness—she chuckles, her face telegraphing both shock and entertainment that this is all being filmed; perhaps it's all part of some grand performance. First-time Housewife and disgraced former NYC socialite Tinsley Mortimer is the only one who tries to intervene, valiantly attempting to defend Morgan before immediately being ganged up on by the other women, who have clearly learned to avoid sticking out a hand when Dorinda is already biting. Tinsley later remarks, "If this is where defending Sonja gets me, I'm gonna stop, 'cause this is getting scary."

Forgive the Carrie-speak, but *I couldn't help but wonder . . . When rage has nowhere to go but out, is it better to take cover or bite back?*

Perhaps we can find the answer in Susan Sharon's story, *SATC* S2E2. When Susan takes Carrie back to her apartment after a fun night out, her husband Richard starts screaming at the girls for making too much noise, eventually demanding Carrie "get the fuck out." She pithily responds, "Goodnight, Grumpy," and heads on her way. Much like Candace Bushnell watching Dorinda scream on *RHONY*, Carrie is just the witness to Susan's husband's rage. She is not the intended target, and she feels unwittingly roped into getting involved, reluctantly admitting that "life's too short" to stay married to someone who yells at you.

Days later, when Carrie is telling the other women at brunch that she may have accidentally encouraged Susan to leave Richard, the women warn Carrie away from intervening. "Practically all the relationships I know are based on a foundation of lies and mutually-accepted delusion," deadpans Samantha, brushing off the blatant verbal abuse.

When Susan *does* leave Richard and seeks refuge on Carrie's couch, Carrie immediately treats the repercussions of her own (very valid) advice as an inconvenience. In retrospect, Carrie's reaction to having to house a distraught Susan for a few days reads as careless, delusional, and cruel: Desperate to relieve herself of her houseguest, Carrie successfully implies that Richard's verbal abuse might be some kind of harmless foreplay. And where does that leave Susan Sharon? Back with her husband, happily letting him abuse a newly-adopted pet dog instead of her. *Hooray*! Out of sight, out of mind! I've never been so glad to be gay.

There is no justice in either franchise. Dorinda's rage does eventually get her fired from *RHONY*, but she reappears in the Bravo universe years later, still drunk, still angry. Susan Sharon also reappears in *And Just Like That* . . . at Big's funeral, ironically the only one to point out that Big was a prick to Carrie when he was alive. She also confesses to Carrie that she's been holding some years-long secret grudge that she finally forgives Carrie for, water under the bridge. "Life's too short," she says to a confused Carrie, who has no memory of their supposed rift. Interestingly, this is reminiscent of another iconic *RHONY* moment—a tearful reunion between two former Housewives and ex-BFFs outside of the funeral of one of their husbands—but there's not enough space in this essay, or in the world, frankly, to get into the Bethenny Frankel/ Jill Zarin relationship dynamics. Let's just say that in the car, on the way to the funeral, fellow Housewife Ramona Singer and our girl Dorinda Medley remark on their friends' years-long grudge that may finally be squashed by the passing of Jill's husband. "Life is too short," Dorinda says, staring off into the middle distance, knowing this pain all too well, even if she's been ignoring the havoc it has wreaked on her and everyone around her for four seasons now.

I would argue that so much of this rage doesn't come from life being too short, but rather life being too long. Dorinda can't cope with living without Richard by her side, so she gets drunk and yells at her friends. Susan Sharon feels she's already logged too many years with her angry husband to start over, so she stays in an abusive marriage. These women are trapped by the rage of middle age, whether consumed by their own rage or the rage of a partner. At least the camera crew is there to witness.

So let's play one last game of Sex-or-RHONY: a woman lets rage consume her life and rob her of joy, while all her friends laugh it off as a big joke or an inconvenience. Is it Sex-or-RHONY? *Both.* And then some. Because somewhere in the Midwest, a gay person watches these episodes for research, thinking she's going to relive her favorite moments of two iconic and influential series and have a laugh about their similarities. But instead, she can't help reflecting on her own childhood in a classic Midwestern home of repressed rage, as she approaches middle age herself, and wonders if life's inevitable disappointments will harden her too. And suddenly, the characters in these episodes seem less like campy queens and more like cautionary tales. How am I doing, trying to make sense of it all? *Not well, bitch.*

# Boyfriend-of-the-Week Brunch Mad Libs

*The girls are sitting at a Manhattan diner, all $$$ on the menu, with LED lighting on the floors and ceiling. Samantha and Carrie sit opposite one another, to enable easy, separate filming. The release of the iDog and the American invasion of Baghdad remain a half-decade away, slowly creeping in on the horizon. It's been a long week for our girls and there are dates to dish about!*

CHARLOTTE: I've been spending time with the most charming man this week . . .

CARRIE NARRATION: Charming was right. His name was [New Testament name] [Old Testament name] [New Testament name] [name of old building in Manhattan] [Roman numeral between II and X]. He had a [type of large apartment] that overlooked the east side of the park and ran a [suburban shrub] fund that brought in $[number] million last year.

CHARLOTTE: *shyly grinning* He rented out the whole [type of alcohol] cellar of the [texture] [farm animal] for our third date.

SAMANTHA: The [repeat texture] [repeat farm animal]? Oh honey, let me tell you, if a man rents out the [repeat texture] [repeat farm animal] for you, you simply must let him rent your [texture] [aquatic animal] between courses.

CHARLOTTE: Samantha! He's not like that. He's sweet and attentive.

SAMANTHA: Well I've been getting a whole other level of attentive from this new man . . .

CARRIE NARRATION: His name was [one-syllable man's name]. In Wall Street steam rooms, he was known as [vicious animal] Eyes, but in Samantha's bed, he was better known as [repeat vicious animal] Tongue.

SAMANTHA: I'm telling you girls, I've never felt anything like it. Every inch of my body wet from his [repeat vicious animal] tongue. And he never breaks contact—like that kid in *A Christmas Story* with the frozen pole! Tongue to body. Man to woman. It's divine.

CARRIE: Never breaks contact? Sweetie, that's not a [repeat vicious animal], that's a [very sticky thing]!

MIRANDA: I once dated a butch—MAN, a MAN who was like that back in college. It was good until the tongue got stuck on my [body part] and we had to walk like that, attached, over to health services.

CARRIE NARRATION: Luckily, Miranda's current infatuation was much more respectful of her personal space. [Two-syllable man name] was a [upper-middle class professional job] who she'd met at a [professional job event] last week. He had just [real estate verb] a [type of real estate property], so there was no danger of him getting too attached to Miranda right away.

MIRANDA: It's just like, god, do I have to spend time with a man to date one? Do I have to kiss him? I mean, I'm an independent woman. It's the 90s. I just want a man who's gonna [gay slur] around a little, fuck me raw, and then leave me alone from [day of the week] until [day of the week before that]. Is that too much to ask?

CARRIE: No sweetie, of course not. So you don't think [repeat two-syllable man's name] could be him?

MIRANDA: He's [synonym for "ok" that betrays resentment]. But there's just no thrill to it.

CHARLOTTE: So now a man can be too clingy AND not thrilling enough. Make up your [body part], Miranda! What can a man do to satisfy you?

MIRANDA: Oh, y'know, just [something disturbing and unsettlingly detailed].

SAMANTHA: I've tried it and let me tell you, girls: with the right man, it can be fabulous.

CARRIE, MIRANDA & CHARLOTTE: Samantha, you [synonym for promiscuous woman]!

CARRIE *grabs Miranda's wrist* Oh shoot. Ladies, I have to run, I'm late for a meeting with my editor. I'll catch you all at [synonym for small] von [baked good]'s [Giuliani policy] fundraiser tonight.

CARRIE NARRATION: As I dashed off into the humid air to cheat on my boyfriend with my married ex, I couldn't help but wonder . . . maybe friends are the real men? Maybe friends, men, and relationships all revolve around one central point? Maybe man friend? But there is a central point. The thing that makes life worth it. The thing that captures our attention and lust for being the center of it: And it's . . .

Me!! Me. 😌 Just being a woman. Having sex AND having my city. And sweetie? That city is New York. That's my man and I love him—almost as much as I love to cheat ;)

CHAE SUNG (성채연)

# Straight Party and the City

Carrie is the perfect straight girl for a bisexual of any gender to go for: a sharp and self-centered sex writer with daring fashion taste who smokes cigarettes on an ice skating rink (kind of iconic, honestly). If I were Sean, better known as the Bisexual Man from "Boy, Girl, Boy, Girl . . ." (S3E4), I too would ignore the red flags of her potential biphobia. I would simply want to bring my hot older girlfriend to my bisexual party: hot girlfriends are famously a hit among bisexuals!

For me, bisexuality was a layover, a brief blip on my way to Gaytown, where I lived for years—planted roots, really. Something compelled me, though, to take a different route back to bi. "I think I want to fuck a man," I announced to my lesbian friends over our meals in Manhattan. "Okay," they said back, tired of my antics, my main character syndrome. "It's really a project about masculinity more than about sexuality," I added. "Okay," they repeated. They said, "I don't really get it, but I support you on your gender and sexuality journey." Ultimately, Carrie Bradshaw was a sort of drag-ified inspiration of mine: like her, I was driven by the pursuit of love; dually—though distinctly—curious about men and the sex I have with them; and at the end of the day, wanting a good story out of it.

This is one way of explaining how I ended up at my first straight party in NYC. It was on a rooftop in Williamsburg. It was BYOB. The girls were wearing crop tops. The boys were drinking beer. I brought a bottle of plum soju. My crop top was from Dickies. It was the birthday of a man I'd been fucking and now was friends with. Sex was still on the table, but not a priority for us: we had done book club together after hooking up a few times; that was better than the sex. What do I bring to a straight party? I wondered beforehand, and then a brilliant idea struck me. Men don't get flowers often, I thought.

"How did y'all meet?" we were asked as I handed him the bouquet. "Oh, we met on Feeld," he answered.

"You met in a field?" they asked incredulously. Oh boy, I thought.

I sanitized the story of our relationship as I rotated through the circles of straight people: we met on a dating app, I told them, during my bicurious era, and now we're friends. The men at the party were curious if I was still bicurious. The women at the party were bicurious. "Mmm, not really," I responded with a shrug. "IDK it's all fluid, but I'm pretty gay." They nodded in vigorous liberal agreement, their interest in me fading. They turned back to their conversations about engagement rings. I disentangled myself from another mansplanation of the FIRE movement, floating through the crowd that was innocuously misgendering me, feeling a little alien, buoyed by the soju only I was drinking.

I was thinking about this while watching the *Sex and the City* bisexual episode, thinking about the parallels between me and Ms. Bradshaw's experience at our respective culture's parties: this anthropological feeling of, damn, people live like this? I was thinking about what is embarrassing about being bisexual: bisexual, as my friend (thanks, Tuck!) characterized it, as being down to date both gay people and straight people (and maybe a secret third thing—what could that be?). That, in this theory, the most embarrassing thing about being bisexual is being attracted to straight people, being around their terribly embarrassing parties. The second most embarrassing thing is probably being attracted to gay people, and their differently embarrassing soirées. The third most embarrassing thing is ultimately being attracted to anyone—how embarrassing.

*A NOTE ON BISEXUAL VISIBILITY: The man whose party I went to is, in fact, bi also.*

At the bisexual party—or, as Carrie calls it, Confused-Sexual-Orientation Land—Carrie kisses Alanis Morissette in slow motion, smoke oozing out of the cigarette in her hand. Organ music, akin to the slightly sluttier sister of the Wedding March, swells and then fades abruptly. After the kiss, we are jolted back into reality: Carrie can't even complete a sentence, her words shattering in her mouth. I mean—after kissing Alanis Morissette, who could? She leaps up and is next seen literally running away from the party, all those flights of stairs in her little breakable heels, physically ghosting a man she had been on at least four dates with. It's a bit of a bisexual awakening with a heavy dose of sexual confusion for sure, and then, a sort of rigid return to straight-ification: a self-induced coma. To Carrie, sleeping with a bisexual man is a layover on her way to Gaytown that she actively did not sign up for. In other words, a bisexual man doesn't exist alone, in a vacuum of straightness. Carrie refuses to be gay, so by her own logic, she can never date bi.

It's easy to see Carrie as alternately tragic or villainous: in both cases, confined by the logic of her heterofatalism; she kisses a woman only in the presence of a man who found her desirable. This is one way to think about straight people as bisexual or to scoff at bisexual women who only date men: they are too scared or too bigoted to even imagine the kind of intimacies that are possible between two people of the "same" gender, the complicated kind of relationships that can unfold. But Carrie is famously unafraid of embarrassing herself for love. Just seven episodes later, she runs down another flight of stairs to escape another beautiful brunette woman: Natasha, the posh young wife Mr. Big is cheating on with Carrie. When Natasha falls down and busts open her lip, Carrie turns back, presses a napkin to the other woman's mouth. She hails a cab, waits in the hospital with her until Big comes. Another episode in which Carrie is bound to another woman, uncomfortably close, by the man she is dating. In this case, though, the man missing from the scene, Carrie offers something different. She stays.

I left the straight party with the apparently straight girl I had been discussing Andrea Long Chu, Saidiya Hartman, and Christina Sharpe with. We sat on the train together for two stops and then she got off. Later, when I asked her about her thoughts on lesbianism, she said, "I'm biding my time." "I respect it," I said, always respectful. In some ways, though, I respected Carrie's experimentation with bisexuality and subsequent full commitment to straightness more. I'm not holding any fantasy that Carrie is bisexual and closeted; rather, I think straightness is just often gay. Each, then, is a choice to endure a different kind of embarrassment, and Carrie, for all her flaws, makes her choice with her full chest. She goes back to Straight City, its cheating and repression, its distance and violence, for one simple reason: she likes the parties better.

SAM SZABO

# Real Actual Episodes of the Television Show *Sex And The City*

Sex and the City
OMG I have nothing to wear to the met Gala!!!
met GALA
OMG Mrs. Met is wearing the same diamond tiara as me!!!
mets
OMG Mrs. Met found out that Mr. Met fingered me at a Natasha Bedingfield concert in 2003! She's pissed off!

Sex and the city
Being a fancy corporate lawyer ain't all it's cracked up to be
LAWS

The violence of late capitalism has become so abstract to me that I can scarcely comprehend my own complicity!

Plus I'm a fucking lesbian!

Sex and the City
Hey Samantha! How was your Ayahuasca retreat?
Terrible

The lines were long, the decor was tacky...

And The ENTITY told me what happens after we die! And it's not good!

SEX and the CITY
I couldn't help but wonder...
Sex and the city
meanwhile...
Stanford can't wait to eat his ice cream cone
SEX and the City

Sex and the city

Sex and the City

Next week on "Sex and the City"...

QUINN KING

# Drag Name: Slayden Shaw

How to do Aidan Shaw drag: oops all denim, distressed to impress. Bolt everything down—grab a handful of brass buttons and fasten them to whatever looks a little loose. Find a leather loveseat that smells like a showroom closet and cut out holes for your arms and head. Measure once, love twice. Aidan Shaw drag should smell like cedar and leaf litter—it should sound like hammers and two middle-aged men mud wrestling. Batten down the wooden window shutters, there is a storm of exes and shopping bags headed upstate with your name on it. Everything you touch turns vintage—leave it as you found it for maximum collector's value. Your ass is a butcher block countertop, and this also perfectly describes your sexuality. When someone doesn't call you back, make that a chair. When they call you faggot, make that a table. Walk onstage like you are about to show someone your secret clubhouse. When the beat drops, move like there is always something in your way that must be avoided or pushed aside. Sink into the floor and leave the wood stove smoldering. Clasp your hands together, sawdust on your collar and the nape of your neck, fabric swatches flagging in your back pocket. Let the people clap.

MB BISCHOFF

# Not So Cosmopolitan

I first saw *Sex and the City* 18 years ago, before I fully understood I was queer and a girl. As a closeted teenager, I cuddled up in front of a tiny TV with my high school girlfriend in the basement of her suburban South Jersey home, dreaming about a life of glamor and sex positivity in the Big Apple. Maybe I should have suspected something when my girlfriend told me that none of the boys she'd dated had wanted to watch the show with her—that I was *different*. Perhaps I should have realized that most 17-year-old straight guys weren't taking "Which *Sex and the City* girl are you?" quizzes on their plastic MacBooks. You live and you learn.

I moved to Manhattan nearly a decade ago, but like many New Yorkers, I've never done many of the activities that tourists flock here for. I swerve around Times Square to avoid the imitation Elmos, I've never climbed to the top of the Statue of Liberty, and I refuse to wait in line with the food influencers for those TikTok croissants. But one fall Friday, I swallowed my pride and embarked on a three-hour-long guided *SATC* tour, hoping to see my city through the eyes of that younger version of myself: the one who'd pondered a life full of cupcakes, Cosmos, and cocks.

Four times a week, On Location Tours runs a "*Sex and the City* Hotspots Tour" of New York City. For $66, they promise to transport you into the "fabulous world of Carrie, Samantha, Charlotte, and Miranda" with a bus tour of 40 real-life locations from the series, where "you'll shop, sip, and spill the tea." I accomplished two out of the three. Not terrible.

After obsessing over what, exactly, a chic transsexual wears to a *Sex and the City* tour, I slipped on a polka-dotted blouse, black pencil skirt, sparkly pink lip gloss, and actual rose-colored glasses, and headed uptown. As soon as I got to Bergdorf Goodman, I wondered if this had all been a terrible mistake. A group of confused women poked their heads around the corner of the department store, looking for our tour guide, while I reclined against the white marble. "Are you here for the *Sex and the City* tour?" they asked me, after looking me up and down a few times. I nodded reassuringly. I made small talk with women of all ages: a mother and her librarian daughter, middle-aged friends who bonded over their shared love of the show, and a group of girlfriends—the straight kind, not a sapphic polycule, sadly—who had previously been on the tour more than a decade ago.

Our guide arrived wielding a frilly pink umbrella, dressed in a red coat and bright yellow pants. Erin (not her real name) was a mid-thirties aspiring-actor from Belgium making money as a tour guide, an elder care worker, and a babysitter—three jobs that are the same job, if you think about it. When she asked for my name to check me in, I realized that I had bought the ticket under my old one. I whispered my birth name, and I could tell she was trying hard to reconcile the name with the outfit.

The fifteen of us boarded a small blue tour bus. "Oh, we only have one man on the tour today," Erin observed. I whipped my head around and was comforted to see that yes, in fact, there was a reluctant but sweet middle-aged man on vacation. He had never seen an episode, but was happy to be anywhere as long as his wife was there too.

Erin introduced herself as a "Charlotte with a Carrie rising," while our driver was a self-identified "Samantha in the sheets, Miranda on the streets." As the bus lurched into midtown traffic, Erin entertained the group with a mix of facts (Samantha's beau Ed had a butt double) and trivia (which of the women had the most sex on the show?).[1] Every time one of us correctly answered a question, she responded with a sultry "Ding, ding, ding" in her best Kim Cattrall impression. The other girls were eating it up.

Erin quickly clocked me as both the only New Yorker and the only trans person in the group, asking me (and only me) for my pronouns. But Erin was not an ally. She hated *And Just Like That*'s "tokenism" and "liberal politics." She misgendered and rolled her eyes at Charlotte's nonbinary child, Rock, and was horrified that she had to see Cynthia Nixon in a strap-on: "It's just too much!" *Too much of a good thing?* I snarked silently.

As we headed downtown, Erin explained that Donald Trump appears in *SATC*, and in a lot of '90s media, only because he owned the Plaza and demanded a cameo in any production filming there. (Of course he did.) When we

---

1. Answer: Charlotte

arrived at the New York Public Library, Erin gave the tour's first and only trigger warning. Except, apparently, she was joking: Instead of offering a useful content note, she pointed out the spot where Mr. Big abandons Carrie on their wedding day, causing a sobbing Carrie to beat him with her bouquet. "Can you feel it in your ovaries?" Erin asked. For whatever reason, I could not.

I was bracing myself for how Erin would address the notoriously transphobic "Cock-a-Doodle-Doo" episode (S3E18), in which Samantha harasses three trans sex workers of color. Erin's attitude was that, while this episode didn't age well, the writers were simply reflecting how the Meatpacking District felt to them at the time. I wanted to grab the mic and explain that NYC only repealed its "Walking While Trans" ban in 2021, and that the transphobia and criminalization of sex work aren't a relic of the past; they still affect our friends and neighbors today. But it wasn't that kind of tour.

The tour used to stop at Babeland, the famous sex shop in the West Village, but I suppose that was just too sexy for a *Sex and the City* tour. (Or maybe the tourists pissed off the staff, who knows?) Instead, we picked up red velvet cupcakes from Magnolia Bakery and made our way to the iconic stoop outside Carrie's apartment—in reality, a multimillion-dollar brownstone now owned by a man who has chained off the steps and yells at tourists to stop Instagramming his house. We took photos anyway; many of the other women pretended to hail a cab, since, unlike the New Yorkers I know, Carrie almost never takes the subway.

The tour concluded at Onieal's, the filming location for Aidan and Steve's SoHo bar, Scout. A round of ungarnished, sickly-sweet Cosmopolitans were served in plastic cups to tourists seemingly unfamiliar with just how strong New York bartenders make their Cosmos. Erin leaned over to surreptitiously buy my drink because she could tell I was "writing a review." (I'd been furiously scribbling in my little notebook throughout the tour.) After a sip of Citron vodka and juice, she went off about how she believes in "innocent until proven guilty" regarding the credible allegations of sexual assault against Chris Noth. She complained about unhoused people wandering onto the set of *AJLT*, and revealed that she daydreams about having a boyfriend who'd beat up guys annoying her at the bar, exactly like Charlotte's belligerent "white knight" Arthur from season 3. As she ranted, I clutched my acrylic coupe ever-tighter.

How can someone who's claimed to have seen *Sex and the City* fifteen times, and has lived in New York City for years, still cling to such regressive views about gender and privilege? Easily, in fact: *Sex and the City* is both a love letter to a particular brand of white, third-wave feminism and an indictment of its limitations. The series broke ground by centering sexuality and independence, but it reflected—and often reinforced—the classist, heteronormative assumptions of its time. It's a portrait of a certain slice of New York: cis, covertly conservative, and oblivious to its own contradictions.

Despite Erin's insistence that "we should be friends," I gulped down my Cosmo and slipped away from the group. As I rode the 6 train home, I reflected on how much I'd outgrown the show's version of NYC. Sure, I have sex, and I'm in the city, but my life—the places I go, the people I love—has room for things that would never fit neatly into Carrie's. (Like, next time I'm on a bus full of women, I'll be riding with a bunch of trans girls to Fire Island for Doll Invasion.)

I couldn't help but wonder how many other '90s kids first caught a glimpse of themselves in *SATC*—and now dance at Bushwick raves sporting new names and cuntier outfits.

HARRON WALKER & ALEX BEDDER

## *Excerpts from*

# "They Have A Very Lovely Life!"

The following are a pair of scenes from our script for *They Have a Very Lovely Life!*, originally staged at Brooklyn queer bar C'mon Everybody on Sept. 17, 2024. It was a retelling-slash-reworking of "Cock-a-Doodle-Do," the infamous "tranny episode" from *Sex and the City*'s third season. Our version pretty much played out like the original episode—with Harron adding narration and stage direction—until Samantha calls the cops on her trans sex worker neighbors and gets conked on the head. In our retelling, as you'll read, Samantha wakes up in a nightmare that shamelessly yet sensuously rips off *A Christmas Carol* (and also kind of *Angels in America*), and it's here where we learn that Samantha has been—GASP!—stealth this whole time.

Our production featured the talents of Macy Rodman (Samantha, Caitlyn Jenner, and others) Joan Summers (Carrie, Susan Stryker, and others), Chiquitita (Charlotte, Robert Moses, and others), and Cherry Jaymes (Miranda, Janet Mock, and others). The stunning Jamie Hood, critic and author of *Trauma Plot* and *How to Be a Good Girl*, tended bar.

• • •

Back in the Meatpacking, Samantha sleeps with a big grin on her face. But then, a thud against her window wakes her.

SAMANTHA

Hmmm?

Another thud. . . then another! Samantha gets out of bed to see eggs flying at her window, yolks running down the pane.

SAMANTHA

Oh! OH!!

Samantha opens the window to reveal Destiny, carton in hand, volleying eggs at her windows.

CARRIE (VO)

He may have gone away a pre-op Transsexual. . . but he came back loaded with eggs. Samantha realized this was one relationship with a man she wouldn't be able to walk away from. . . because this man. . . was half-woman.

DESTINY

NOW WHO'S LAUGHING BITCH?!

Destiny chucks an egg. It hits Samantha in the face. She falls backwards to the floor and is knocked out cold.

Blackout.

When she wakes, the apartment is eerily dark. There's no longer any moonlight and a strange mist covers the floor.

Samantha hears footsteps approaching her apartment door. Moaning. The sounds of chains dragging on the floor.

SAMANTHA

Mmmm. Kinky.

The door bursts open to reveal a ghost. A *male* ghost!

SAMANTHA

Well, *hello*.

ROBERT MOSES

(spooky-ooky ghost voice)

Hello, it's me. New York's greatest villain: Robert Moses!

A flash of lightning, the sound of thunder!

ROBERT MOSES

As penance for my sins against the city, I have to spend all of eternity helping. . . build community!

SAMANTHA

Okay, it's getting a little La MaMa in here. And I'm looking for a *La PAPA* if you get my drift—

ROBERT MOSES

SILENCE!

Robert Moses points at Samantha.

ROBERT MOSES

Samantha Jones! You have sinned against your sisters. You have turned your back on your community.

SAMANTHA

What community?

ROBERT MOSES

You have turned your back on the TRANS community!

SAMANTHA

From what I've heard, so have you. Guess after you bulldoze a couple of neighborhoods and fuck the city, you're too good to admit to getting fucked in the ass. You, Ed Koch, Roy Cohn. . . I know all your tea.

ROBERT MOSES

And I know *yours*!

SAMANTHA

(gasp)

ROBERT MOSES

Tonight you will be visited by three spirits: The ghosts of Transgender Past—

Samantha rolls her eyes.

ROBERT MOSES

Fine. The Ghost of *Transsexual* Past.

Samantha flashes her signature thumbs up.

ROBERT MOSES

The Ghost of Transsexual Present, and the Ghost of Transsexual Future.

SAMANTHA

So, we're doing a *Christmas Carol*?

ROBERT MOSES

Yes.

SAMANTHA

Okay, sure. Why not? If I'm not having a sex dream, I guess I'll settle for whatever this is.

The ghost of Robert Moses begins to fade away. . .

ROBERT MOSES

Prepare the way! The great work begins! I hear the approach of the first spirit now!!

Thunder rumbles. The apartment shakes. Samantha holds on for dear life as the ceiling begins to crack open. Light and clouds spill into the room.

The ceiling breaks open with the sounds of trumpets. Then, nothing. The light and clouds dissipate.

Samantha stands up and looks confused. Then, a totally normal woman starts to climb down out of the crack. She makes her way down to the floor, stands, and combs sheetrock out of her hair.

SUSAN STRYKER

Hi. It’s me. Susan Stryker.

SAMANTHA

But you’re just some lady!

SUSAN STRYKER

I know! Anyway, Samantha, I hate to begin today’s lecture by disclosing another woman’s transgender status, thereby participating in a violent act that has historically levied such harm against the community writ large.

Susan dims the lights and rolls out a slide projector. She picks up the clicker and clicks to the first slide, which reads, “Transgender History 101.”

In an inset starburst in the bottom right corner of the slide sits an image of Susan’s book, *Transgender History*. Beside it, a line of text reads, “Audiobook now available on Audible, Spotify, and Google Play.”

SUSAN STRYKER

So many women have had their lives, even their livelihoods wholly upended upon being forcibly outed. Take Tracey Norman or April Ashley, both of them successful models in the latter half of the 20th century until the facts of their respective medical histories became, against their will, public knowledge.

Susan clicks to the next slide, which shows three crudely drawn stick-figure women with triangle skirts. A speech bubble shouted by all three reads in all caps, "OUTING SOMEONE IS BAD!"

SUSAN STRYKER

And then there's Caroline Cossey, whose star rose under the mononymous pseudonym "Tula," the one-time Bond girl-turned-trans rights advocate who—

SAMANTHA

Yeah, yeah, sorry to those men. But what does any of this have to do with a beautiful, biological woman like myself?

SUSAN STRYKER

That's precisely what I'm getting to! For you see, well. . . I hope you'll forgive me for saying so, for "spilling the T" as one might say in the vernacular, but Samantha. . . You are transgender.

SAMANTHA

No, I'm not! How dare you?!

SUSAN STRYKER

You're right. Excuse me. Transsexual.

SAMANTHA

That's better. But Susan. . . who told you?

SUSAN STRYKER

The author of *Transgender History* knows all.

Susan clicks to the next slide. A bunch of graphs and charts and unreadably small text appears. The only part Samantha can make out is the large-font, bolded title: "WHITE FLIGHT & GENTRIFICATION IN POSTWAR AMERICA"

SUSAN STRYKER

I know that you, like many white Americans your age, reversed course on the previous generation's collective exodus from our nation's various urban metropoli and charted a course for the city from which your white flighter parents had previously white-fled. Hoping to escape the provincial bigotries and structural oppressions that would have otherwise limited your autonomy in your hometown, you arrived in Manhattan in the early 1970s—

Susan clicks to the next slide. We see a faded, washed out picture of what looks to be a gay guy stepping off a bus with a suitcase in each hand. Strands of synthetic hair in different shades spill out from the suitcases' seams.

SAMANTHA

Three bucks. Two bags. One messy little crossdresser.

SUSAN STRYKER

Ah, yes. The figure of the crossdresser, one of my favorite archetypes from post-war transgender history.

Susan clicks to the next slide. We see a still from that episode of *Transparent* where Moppa goes to crossdresser camp.

SUSAN STRYKER

Virginia Prince, *Transvestia*, Casa Susanna. . . You know, as Jules Gill-Peterson, the historian and author of *Histories of the Transgender Child* and *A Short History of Trans Misogyny*, once observed, the suburban postwar crossdress—

SAMANTHA

Back to me, Susan!

SUSAN STRYKER

Right, apologies!

Susan clicks to the next slide. A young Samantha, nearly nude in a rhinestone bikini and matching nipple covers, poses onstage in a dingy nightclub.

SUSAN STRYKER

After moving to the city, you started earning a modest income as a showgirl at the Peppermint Lounge and the Gilded Grape, where you performed what would become your signature burlesque number, which featured freeform scatting accompanied by an upright bass.

SAMANTHA

And the town never knew such a hullabaloo. . .

SUSAN STRYKER

You also used to walk the stroll right outside this window, engaging in the highly criminalized labor that is street-based sex work—

SAMANTHA

You mean selling my ass?

SUSAN STRYKER

Yes! But you wanted more. You wanted—

SAMANTHA

A pussy. I'd never wanted a cock less in my life. . .

SUSAN STRYKER

So you grabbed a pen and paper and wrote a letter to Harry Benjamin, the father of contemporary transgender medicine as we know it.

Susan clicks to the next slide. We see a crudely drawn stick figure of a man, smiling a simple smile. Beside him reads the word "COMPLICATED" with an arrow pointing to his head.

SUSAN STRYKER

He wrote back immediately, urging you to travel down to Johns Hopkins posthaste.

SAMANTHA

Because I was so passing? The most beautiful woman he'd ever seen?

SUSAN STRYKER

No! Because you were the, quote, "worst case of homosexuality [he'd] ever seen, posing the greatest threat to American public decency since Mae West went over Niagara Falls in a barrel, totally nude." That's what Dr. Benjamin had written in your file, which I uncovered many years ago during my postdoctoral research. Gender-affirming care on an informed consent basis, you see, is a thoroughly modern phenomenon. In the late 1970s, back when you completed your medical transition, the primary goal of medical practitioners like Dr. Benjamin was not to help trans people transition into their true genders but to eliminate gender-nonconformity. The goal was assimilation, so for some, particularly those subaltern subjects who didn't pass—

SAMANTHA

I get it, Susan. I downed that bottle of Premarin and had Dr. Benjamin turn my outie into an innie.

SUSAN STRYKER

And in doing so, found yourself able to slip into straight nightlife, no questions asked.

Susan clicks to her final slide, which shows Samantha with crimped hair, neon pink blush, and a Mugler power suit, lying on a pile of cash.

SUSAN STRYKER

Before long you had built an impressive career as an upstart music publicist. You discovered Madonna at Danceteria, you worked for George Michael shortly before he co-founded Wham! and convinced him to stay in the closet. You even ran into RuPaul in line for drinks one time when Blondie played CBGB and explained to him that fracking would be a great investment.

SAMANTHA

Classic Samantha!

SUSAN STRYKER

But what transpired in the decades since that pre-Giuliani epoch of yore? How did Samantha Jones, the transvestite sex worker fleeing police violence, become the purportedly cisgender penthouse owner dialing 9-1-1? I leave you now, Samantha, in the care of another: the Spirit of Transsexual Present. . .

Susan adjusts her glasses, waves goodbye, and wheels her slide projector out of Samantha's apartment and into the hallway, squeaking as she goes.

Samantha hears the sound of the static and the comforting “bwonnnng” of the HBO title card. . . then a delightful, jazzy tune that makes her want to strut down Park Avenue.

She turns around and someone is sitting down, silhouetted in the glow of her TV. Displayed are the opening credits. . . to *Sex and the City*.

SAMANTHA

And who, may I ask, are you?

JANET MOCK

I'm the ghost of Transsexual Present, of course. . .

The beautiful woman stands up and turns around.

SAMANTHA

JANET MOCK!?!

JANET MOCK

That's right. I'm here toda—

SAMANTHA

Are you here to show me how the choices I made today are a direct result of my class, whiteness, and—

JANET MOCK

We're not doing that. I'm just here to watch *Sex and the City* with you. Don't interrupt Janet Mock when she's watching her favorite show, okay? Well, come on, sit down!

Janet Mock pulls one hand from behind her back to reveal a bottle of champagne. Samantha smiles. Janet Mock pulls out her other hand to reveal ANOTHER bottle of champagne. Samantha jumps up and down, cheering!

They sit down and clink glasses of bubbly together as we zoom in on the television screen where we see that. . . Carrie is waiting outside the Boathouse in Central Park, calling Miranda on a payphone.

• • •

From here, we spend several minutes watching Carrie and Big meet for lunch, fall in a lake, rehash their breakup in terry cloth robes, etc. Janet Mock loves it. Later in Manhattan, Samantha is paid a visit by the Ghost of Transsexual Future . . .

• • •

Carrie closes the window. SLAM!

Suddenly, she is gone. Janet Mock is gone. Samantha is alone in the dark apartment.

SAMANTHA

Carrie? Janet Mock? Trans History Lady? Anyone??

She looks around. She notices the answering machine, a single blinking red light in the dark.

She slowly walks over, and presses play. The voice of the final spirit begins speaking to her. . .

CAITLYN JENNER

Hey, sis! It's me, Caitlyn. They said they needed someone from the future and I volunteered because, let's just say I'm a fan. I never missed a big *Sex and the City* Sunday. You were a real inspiration for good ole Cait here! And trust me, you think your life might be one way. . . that it'll never change. . . AND JUST LIKE THAT. . . BOOM, Annie Leibovitz is saying "CHIN UP" and you're on the cover of *Vanity Fair*!

Yeah, so in the future you and Carrie are no bueno. It's real sad. You two fall out and you move to London. Basically they just kinda ADR you in every once in a while for a phone call.

Sometimes they get Sarita Choudhury to come do your thing and everyone loves it because they miss you so much.

Also, Sarita Choudhury. . . what a gorgeous gal. I mean, just really *stunning*. I love *Mississippi Masala*, you ever see *Mississippi Masala*?

So yeah, it's all very woke. Miranda blows up her life to date a nonbinary comedian who isn't funny. She's also kind of alcoholic now?

And Charlotte. . . well, Charlotte's doing pretty well. She also has a nonbinary, her kid uses they/them pronouns. You're not gonna know what this means, but there's a lot of they/thems.

So yeah, what else, what else. . . Big gets MeToo'd and dies on a Peloton. . . oh!! Stanford becomes a monk. Carrie is back with Aidan! It's all pretty kooky crazy.

But yeah, you're not there. No more Sam Jones! It's basically like you never existed. Like you were erased from herstory. . .

Samantha wakes up on the floor in a cold sweat. She rushes to the window. The sun is just rising and Destiny is smoking a cigarette on the street.

SAMANTHA

Hey, diva! What day is it?

DESTINY

Bitch, it’s been 10 minutes.

SAMANTHA

Thank god! Listen, I am so sorry about all of this. . . but I think I know a way to make it up to you.

# MATTIE LUBCHANSKY

***SAMANTHA JONES, TRANNY PASS ENFORCEMENT AGENCY*** ***mattie lubchansky***

YEAH, I'VE GOT A PASS TO SAY THE WORD "*TRANNY*" AS MUCH AS I LIKE.
TRANNY. *TRANNY.* BEAUTIFUL.

WELL, THAT ISN'T FAIR. HOW COME?

IT'S SIMPLE, HONEY. I'M AN *HONORARY* DOLL!
BUT WHY?!

BECAUSE I'M A HOT SLUT AND A BITCH BUT IN AN INTERESTING WAY!
GOODBYE!
LUB

AMY ZIMMERMAN

# Aidan Is My Friend

People always assume I became a bartender because my mother is a drunk. (And, let's face it, her mother and her mother's mother before that—a long line of rheumy-eyed, pink-nosed women, going all the way back to our matriarch, who I imagine clutching a bottle of her birthright in the hull of some cursed ship out of Belfast, claiming seasickness to mask her morning hurl.) But really, I love booze because it's holy. That smell alone: purifying, clean. It takes me back to my childhood: the hydrogen peroxide rag my ma would clamp on all our cuts, the wound under her hands pounding like a heartbeat, stigmata stinging into resurrection. Or the huge tubs of cleaning solution the nuns would make us carry to the entrance of our school, Our Lady of Sorrows Catholic Academy. Every morning, Christ's youngest soldiers fought a battle against filth, getting down on hands and khaki'd knees to wipe away whatever grime, gum, shit and piss had built up while we were sleeping. It was a miracle how well the cleaning solution worked, both on the ancient stone and on our pliant little brains, inducing giggles, euphoria, and visual hallucinations. By simply pressing a soaked paper towel to my face, I could at any time escape my present situation. Leave behind the loud street, my wise-cracking classmates, the curious stares of passing kids whose schools didn't require uniforms or manual labor. Ascend to somewhere higher, pure white and heaven-scented.

I often reminisced about knocking myself out with cleaning products when joining Miranda and her friends for dinner. After the first few meals, I learned that my participation in the conversation was not only unnecessary, but actively discouraged. Carrie didn't want to hear when she was acting crazy, Samantha didn't want any notes on her sex puns, and Charlotte was not receptive to my suggestion that she find a nicer group of friends; *no one* wanted to talk about the New York Knicks. It was similar, actually, to my dynamic with the nuns: how they would order me to go somewhere and do something, then stand around chatting and laughing to themselves like I didn't even exist. I was sitting at one of these dinners, wondering how effectively I could lobotomize myself with a corkscrew, when Aidan walked in the door. It wasn't love at first sight; time didn't slow down—although maybe it did, just a little bit, when he smiled and ran silver-ringed fingers through his hair.

What I came to like most about Aidan—what I found most attractive, if I'm being honest—was his carpentry. I've always admired competency; like Miranda, who knows the law so well that she can use it for good or evil, or my cousin Finn, who cashed out on GameStop in 2021 and moved to the Bahamas. Aidan's skills were different, though. He didn't memorize or read; he had a physical kind of knowledge, where muscle memory meets intuition. Like Carmelo Anthony or

Carlos Santana. Not that I didn't respect Aidan's mind too . . . But fuck, I'll admit it: I just really liked to watch him touch that wood.

The first time I thought about sucking Aidan off was at that first dinner. I wanted to follow him into the bathroom, shove him into a stall, and hear the noise he'd make when I dropped to the floor: surprised, definitely, maybe even offended. But soon he'd be moaning, and then he'd be cursing, and then I'd get to feel those calloused fingers rough in my own hair. Miranda was so locked into her conversation she probably wouldn't even notice I was gone; she'd absentmindedly pick the fleck of dried cum from the corner of my mouth later without thinking twice. Something about that thought was really hot: how much I'd make him care, and how little she ever would.

It went on like this for years, just a low-level crush I kept in my back pocket, picking it up whenever I was bored behind the bar or stuck between subway stations. The first time we played hoops together, at the Bay Ridge courts where they don't laugh at white guys so much, I thought about pulling down the elastic band of Aidan's gym shorts and licking the sweat from his asscrack. When we started scoping out spaces for our very own bar, I fantasized about leaning him over every pool table, eyes closed and lips wrenched open by my fingers, his spit darkening the felt.

It would've all stayed a fantasy if it wasn't for what happened at the opening night of Scout. For months before, I'd watched Aidan suffer; Carrie had really done a number on him. Personally, I didn't get it. She was a good-looking girl, sure, but she couldn't cook, was way more neurotic than she let on, and her credit score was shit. Still, my boy Aidan loved that black hole of attention and validation wrapped in a skin-tight dress; he loved her when she chain-smoked and even when she cheated, those expensive stilettos drilling deeper and deeper into his heart. When they broke up, he became the walking wounded: whiskey breath, always on the verge of tears, and losing weight faster than a butcher during Lent. It killed me to see Aidan—always quick to laugh, content with just a beer or two, happily licking fried chicken grease from his fingers-Aidan—like this. And then she came waltzing into our bar in a little black dress, and with one look at Aidan's face I knew that all had been forgiven.

He looked so good that night too, his fresh-pressed suit showing off that new body of his, lithe and just a little mean, his hair cut short like he was going into battle. I watched him following Carrie outside like a bloodhound, pressing up against the smell of her, false scent of home: nicotine, gin, expensive perfume. I knew that he would catch her in the end. So that night, high on our success and a few shots deep, I walked up to him when we were closing. Everyone had gone home by then, and I was giving the place a final sweep while Aidan waited, leaning against the wall like some teen movie heartthrob. Afraid to look him in the eye, I watched the bob of his Adam's apple as I came closer and closer, finally crossing the line of all plausible deniability, my boots against his boots, his clean and holy breath mixing with my own.

"What are you—" Aidan exhaled, but I knew he was just following a script, saying what he thought he was supposed to. So I put my hand on his waist, warm and just a little wet beneath his jacket, and pressed my cock against his until I felt it stir. "It's just me, man," I said. "It's Steve." I watched his eyes move quickly over my wire-rimmed glasses, the big ears I've always been self-conscious of, the stubble of my chin. My lips, parted. Aidan closed the small space between us in an instant, turning me around and up against the wall, moaning. We rubbed up against each other, laughing one moment and then so serious we could barely breathe, let alone speak: my cock in his hand, so rough and warm; then, his cock full and leaking in my mouth.

Afterwards, we lay naked together on a makeshift bed of clothes and dishrags, his leg thrown over mine and my hand tucked in his waist. We talked for hours, pausing every so often to make out, or just to laugh at the sheer absurdity of us, the unexpected joy of this. It was just so easy, like it's always been, like I always knew it would be. Unlike Carrie, I loved Aidan's laid-back, hippie style, his homebody ways; I missed that extra meat on his thighs and waist and stomach. Unlike Miranda, Aidan could remember all of my teams and always asked about my Ma. He didn't rag on my old gym shorts; he loved my one and only ball. This: our bar, our bodies, passing sleep and sex and laughter back and forth, made so much more sense than our girlfriends' alien world, where people spent $100 on brunch and $600 on shoes, where relationships ran on passive aggression and unspoken rules, and where ladies wore fur freaking coats to the freaking ball game. Aidan and I returning to that world, where neither of us was fully seen or loved, felt as unimaginable as it did inevitable. I closed my eyes and resolved to stay in this perfect moment for as long as it lasted; it reminded me of that childhood high, the momentary heaven I could only reach by sniffing cleaning supplies. Just a little longer, I would plead; don't send me back just yet.

It never happens again, at least not like that. Every so often when we were out to dinner with our girlfriends, Aidan would grab my ass at the coat check, or I'd give him a quick hand job in the bar bathroom on a particularly slow night. Then Aidan and Carrie broke up again, Aidan moved away, and before I knew it we were exchanging dick pics in lieu of holiday cards, an annual reminder that I didn't dream the whole thing up. Decades passed. Miranda turned gay, which made me wonder if I could too; I got back into shape, protein shakes and punching bags, and let myself imagine it: how I would do things right this time, take him out to dinner, lead him slowly to my bed. When I hear from my ex that Aidan and Carrie are back together after all these years, I'm disappointed but not surprised. When they come to visit my new spot in Coney Island, I tell myself to be grateful for even this: beautiful Aidan eating my food, drinking my beer, giving me his widest smile. I watch him bright against the ocean, my prodigal crush, a constant undercurrent beneath all of my days, my entire life. I force myself to smile back; after all, Aidan is my friend.

SARAH ESOCOFF

# True Love

This is a drawing of Aidan fucking Steve. I have received a lot of feedback that Steve would top, but I disagree and think I'm right.

ADRIAN MATIAS BELL

# Total Charlotte

I'm a Charlotte. I knew it as soon as I saw her. It was something about the way she carried herself: her strange, prim tenseness. While the other girls were comfortable gabbing about sex, Charlotte was simultaneously pulled in and pushed away, as if an invisible magnet inside her was constantly flipping around. She was like me—and not just because she was also three years away from converting to Judaism. She was a faggot, too.

Although we as queer people can generally agree, at least in mixed company, that media representation is good, there is something intoxicating about a fictional world in which you will absolutely never see yourself represented. (This is arguably what took *And Just Like That . . .* off the rails, but that's another essay.) Aside from the nightmarish third-season finale, which relies on Black trans women as a punchline, trans people are completely invisible in the original *Sex and the City.* In some ways, I am happiest as a viewer when *SATC* is less diverse, because it affords itself fewer chances to fuck up. It provides all the fly-on-the-wall glee of being invited to the bachelorette party without the devastation of someone misgendering you while looking you dead in the eye.

But poor Charlotte: she's stuck at this party—the party that is her entire life—and it's never going to end. She doesn't even want to be here. She wants to marry a nice, rich man and start a nice, traditional family. This gender of "perfect single woman" is too tight, but if she trades it for "perfect wife and mother," she might not be able to take it off. But what else is she supposed to wear? Nothing? You can't do that. There are *rules.*

I didn't spend nearly as much of my life in the closet as I could have. I'm very lucky for that. But when I was in there, I performed my gender very similarly to Charlotte. I was a Good Girl, both aesthetically and morally. I liked boys who were kind, sensitive, and maybe even a little bit gay. What could be wrong with that? I was an ally.

In Charlotte, I see my old gender: its rich rewards and its deep, secret anger. There's a reason why Charlotte is the most judgmental of the girls, and the most uptight. But what else can she be? She's not a lesbian, as her failed friendship with the power lesbians proves (S2E6). She won't abide by bisexuality (S3E4), and nonbinary identity confuses and frightens her (*AJLT* S1E5). And a gay man? Charlotte panics: her eyes grow wide, and she breaks into a frightened smile. Oh, that's ridiculous! Oh, you are just so *funny*!

Yet faggotry keeps finding her. Charlotte has tighter connections to gay masculinity than any of the other women. She falls for perfectly wonderful fruity men (S2E11), then dumps them because they're scared of mice. She and Anthony become phantom limbs for each other, each living the gender that feels forbidden to the other. (Dual egg situation? Let me know.)

Charlotte is profoundly afraid of her own gender and sexuality, but the people around her share her fears. She's afraid of enjoying a vibrator too much (S1E9) because it might make her like straight sex less; Carrie and Miranda, similarly fearful, come to her apartment to confiscate the Rabbit. Yes, Charlotte wants to fulfill her fantasy of being a woman content in her particular version of womanhood, even and especially if it's no fun. But her friends want this from her too.

When I first watched the infamous drag king episode (S3E4, the same episode where we learn the gang hates bisexuality), I was surprised by how emotionally affecting it was. Charlotte gets so flustered by Baird, photographer of drag kings, that the cause must be deeper than his mere hotness. As she distances herself from him and his roguish suggestion that gender is socially constructed, you can see the very edges of her own gender starting to fray.

It's the perfect gentle forced-masc fantasy, and one of the only times Charlotte wins a man with something other than her usual poised femininity. "I'm not butch," she insists, as the reason she can't pose for Baird. "I'm really bad at math and I can't change a tire to save my life." Baird encourages her, later, in the mirror: "You're a hot guy . . . you can get any woman you want. You eat guys like me for lunch." But of course, Charlotte doesn't want any woman. She wants him, and herself.

(Side note: Baird has to be a stealth trans guy, right? He roams around the country taking people's photos in drag and cracking eggs left and right, doesn't he? I get that they had to make him a cis guy, but that was kind of a wild choice, wasn't it? But good for me and the tens, if not dozens, of Charlotte Transfag Truthers out there.)

Even though it's played for laughs, Charlotte beholding herself in drag and getting horny about it is beautiful to me. It is one of the few moments in the entire series when Charlotte genuinely sees herself as desirable. It also might be the only time her capacity for desire lines up with that feeling. Blanchard be damned: the first time I tried on a binder or wore a packer, the first place I looked was a mirror. Sure, I felt that nice sense of belonging we tell cis people about. But I also felt a sense of wild desire: for myself, for masculinity, but most of all for another world and another life that I suddenly sensed could open, even to me.

I want to know about the world where the gay man trapped in Charlotte's body is let out again, this time for good. Her actual character arc, while artfully done and featuring my beloved Kyle MacLachlan, is a letdown by comparison: just another death spiral into the failures of gender normativity, followed by a sweet romance with the (iconic, let's be clear) Harry Goldenblatt. But I want to know about the version of Charlotte who leaves the party early and never puts on the gender of "perfect single woman" again. I want to know about the version of Charlotte whose egg gets cracked by other gay men, who is first called a man by other men and a fag by other fags. I want Charlotte to know what I know now. I want her to know she doesn't have to be mad anymore.

I'm writing this because I still can't point to any fictional media that adequately explains the transfag experience. Even with the massive blessing and curse of increased trans visibility over the last decade, transfagginess remains elusive, interstitial. Maybe that one five-second gag in *Ghost of Girlfriends Past* where a charming young trans man appears in a lineup of Matthew McConaughey's ex-lovers. Maybe that one hag in Larry Kramer's *Faggots* who dresses like a boy and enjoys fucking gay men. I don't know. Who has us in their minds? Do we look hot in there?

After all this time, looking for other transfags in media feels like walking down the street in New York City, locking eyes with stranger after stranger, trying to find someone you know. *Have we met before? What about you?* Eventually, you'll ask anyone, just to have something to say. And you'll realize, when someone tries to avoid looking back, that you know exactly who they are.

# Recession

Before the recession, I saw Samantha
take off her shirt on TV:

hands grabbing shirt on opposite hips,
pulling up for a big splash of early aughts'

impossible tummy. In my bedroom mirror I
practiced taking off my shirt with blank eyes

my younger self's ideal is a frail lamb of
weight loss weighed down in gold ornaments;

now I am the SeaWorld whale
and the trainer he pulled under:

a thousand pounds of muscle
drifting in a pool of resentments,

hunger personified when I remember
what my body is for,

I pull that frail mammal down
until there isn't any thrashing left.

MALACHI BOLING

# Mr. Big Tumor

*12:49 AM, April 27, 2024*—Noah and I head to the ER. He has a sharp pain in his stomach that keeps getting worse—appendicitis, maybe? The doctors tell us it is not appendicitis but rather a large tumor blocking his intestines. Suddenly we are very afraid.

The way to treat an intestinal blockage is with a thick tube that is shoved down your nose into your stomach. The tube sucks everything up and allows your intestines to relax. I have it on good authority that it is quite painful going in, and very uncomfortable to have lingering inside you. They biopsy the tumor and tell us we'll get the results in a few weeks. We wait.

*3 PM, April 30*—E! starts replaying *Sex and the City* from the beginning (having moments prior concluded their previous *SATC* marathon), and Carrie asks the fateful question, "Were women in New York really giving up on love?"

We have to know. *Were* women in New York really giving up on love? It's great hospital viewing, because nothing ever really changes: Carrie is always going to be a monster. Their problems are fake: "What if I kiss a 23-year-old and I like it but he doesn't have toilet paper at home?" There is a genocide happening, and I don't know if my husband has cancer. I feel insane. All I can do is be at the hospital for the duration of visiting hours. All I can do is make myself believe that everything will be okay. Has Carrie ever experienced grief? True fear?

*Sex and the City* is a gift: something to talk about with visitors other than the horror we are experiencing. A friend who just watched it warns us that "it's really problematic," and "there's this episode where Carrie dates a bisexual . . ."

In a New York City that has become the size of half a hospital room, we want to see the New York City of fantasy, one that we have never glimpsed in our years here, one that had never existed for us and probably not for anybody. So we watch the worst person in the world (Carrie Bradshaw) make terrible decisions, learn nothing, and smoke indoors. Watching, we wait days in the hospital for Noah's stomach to decompress. Then we go home, and wait more for the results of the biopsy. We learn it's not cancer—just a close relative. Did you know that cancer has a cousin?

*3:51 AM, July 22*—Noah wakes up in pain, with a fever. This time we have no hope of appendicitis; we go straight to the urgent care at Noah's cancer hospital. We find out within a few hours of arriving that the tumor has torn a hole inside of Noah's intestines, causing them to leak into his body. Gallons of antibiotics flood his system by IV. Painkillers, saline solution, potassium. The things necessary to keep him alive.

By 10 AM we are in a hospital room, and by 11 AM we are once again watching *Sex and the City* on E!

*11:37 AM, July 22—in an unnamed group chat*

Me: Oh my god we just got to the bisexual episode of sex and the city

Noah: I kinda like it cause Carrie doesn't deserve happiness

Me: But carrie taking away from this the question "has the opposite sex become obsolete?" is so typical
Like always just the most inane question

Noah: I also love the fiction that the artist behind the drag king photography show is a straight man

Me: "Gender is an illusion. . . . Sometimes a very beautiful one" a straight man says looking at Carrie

Noah: Okay but Carrie has maybe the most clocky energy of any cis woman on tv in this era

Me: Every woman has a male inside of her

Sara: the duality of biologically prescribed gender . . .

Me: To which the virginal one says "I can't even change a tire"

Sara: It's wild that this was probably considered radical and cool in the 90s and not an insane way to think about how either gender or sexuality work

Me: This episode is insane
"Do I kiss better than a guy?"

Noah's fever continues to rise; his pain is excruciating even with the morphine. The surgeon tells us impassively that they will probably do surgery tomorrow, that we can expect them to remove several feet of intestine. At some point when I am not in the room, Noah writes a document to read in case he dies.

*July 23*—Today Noah's fever continues to climb; it peaks somewhere above 105°. On E! they air "Sex and Another City" (S3E14), in which Samantha covers her body in sushi (how?) and waits for some guy to show up. He doesn't come. She is disgraced. I have the idiotic thought that it was strange how much time the writers spent humiliating Samantha with food.

Noah is scheduled for emergency surgery at 2 or 3 PM, but it is rescheduled to 4 PM, then 7 PM. It is 8 PM and somehow I am texting another friend about *Sex and the City*.

*8:42 PM, July 23—in a group chat called "Gay Guy Sunday"*

Me: We've been watching sex and the city on E
When Noah is awake

Ray: You mean the edited and censored SatC?
Sex sans the City?

(I should have corrected him "You mean sexless and the city")

Me: Yes
Literally the only kind I've ever seen
Never seen it unedited lmao

Ray: to you, it's about a nice group of young woman making it in the big city
Samantha must have such a small part for you

We sit in the dark as Noah's fever continues, impossibly, to rise. Finally, just after 11 PM, they take Noah to the OR. After three harrowing hours pretending to feel calm, I receive a call from the surgeon. Noah didn't die. The surgery went better than they expected. She used gallons of liquid to wash out the infection. She removed all the tumor that she could see.

*October 20*—I thought that this essay would be funny. I'm not sure why. I've only seen *Sex and the City* in my grandparent's basement and hospital rooms. *Sex and the City* was always on, my eternal visiting hours companion as I sat beside hospital beds, two and a half miserable weeks, bookending a summer of torturous uncertainty. Was Noah dying? Will we get to have children? Will either of us be okay again? Can I, not known for my emotional acuity, actually be of any use? But, I tell myself, I handled it better than Carrie would. Carrie would have left. I stayed, even when I wanted to run away.

I should probably never watch *Sex and the City* again. I can hear the crinkle of a plastic bed behind me; I can feel the heat of Noah's fever; I can hear him asking the nurses, panicked, if he has sepsis as I think about Aidan drawing a bath for Carrie and her acting fucking weird about it. When Noah was in the hospital, I felt fine. I felt in control, orderly. But when I think about Aidan trying to understand why Carrie won't love him, I feel everything that I very efficiently did not feel the summer that Noah almost, but did not, die. *Sex and the City* is a key, and it is one that I will lose.

K3

# Lay Down the Law

They say nothing lasts forever; dreams change, trends come and go, but Miranda on my ass never goes out of style. The artist remains anonymous, but if you're lucky enough, maybe one day you'll find out who it is. ;P

# Help! My Miranda Is a Man! (Duh!)

If your Miranda Hobbes has recently told you he is a transfag named Hobbes (yes, just Hobbes), you're not alone. Realising he is a transfag is a normal part of any Hobbes overcoming his inexplicable, yet undeniable, bad vibes that puzzlingly persist despite achieving every conceivable marker of beauty and success.

The good news is, you now have an answer to why your Hobbes:

- Wanted to dress like a dapper little boy (lesbian?) but couldn't bring himself to date women (he tried repeatedly, but could only ever get as far as a non-binary transmasc)

- Gave off "out of place in womanhood" vibes despite looking like Cynthia Nixon

- Gravitated towards trans partners in a non-chasery way (e.g., Che, Steve)

- Felt such profound empathy with Steve's anguish over having fewer than two testicles, that he risked getting pregnant to make Steve feel better

- Met Carrie because he started dysphoria-crying in a changing room

- And more!

We know you have questions for your Hobbes, but we suggest you let this pamphlet answer them and wait until your new Gay Best Friend is ready for you to hag out with him.

**Wait, what do you mean trans partners, e.g., Steve???**
Steve is obviously a man of transgender history. He is so broke because his phalloplasty left him with insurmountable debt. While this is a sad reminder of the structural inequalities that transgender people face, on the upside, Steve is so masc that God gave him the power to produce functional semen after his dick got finished up, so there are no plot holes created by this revelation.

**Is Hobbes his new given name? So he's Hobbes Hobbes? Or is he just going by his last name now? How does that work?**
Good question. Hobbes approached naming himself with the same strategy he used for his son, Brady Hobbes. (That is, use a last name as a first name.) Hobbes stands by his convictions pretty firmly, so he's too embarrassed to change

it now, but he will have to address this at some point, yeah. Don't bring it up.

**Hobbes stopped dressing like a drag king decades ago. Where is this coming from?**
Have you ever heard of resignation syndrome?

**How long has this been going on? Why didn't he tell me sooner? Did he think I wouldn't accept him? How can I be a better ally?**
Sweet Charlotte, your love and acceptance is like a laser beam, and Hobbes hates to be in the spotlight. These unchangeable aspects of your personality cause a delightful friction that makes for excellent television.

That said, should you have been able to tell? No. Even though Hobbes has phoned in "really busy at work" or "still recovering from laryngitis" to over nine months of brunch at this point (which are up there with "gynecomastia" and "it's a sports bra" in the Trans Guy White Lies Hall of Fame, by the way), I cannot fault you for taking him at his word. That is simply a consequence of your propensity for literal thinking—which you are now self-aware about because you've realised you're autistic! Good for you.

No, this was not an issue caused by a lack of ally knowledge. When you came to pick Hobbes up for the Late-Diagnosed Autistic Women Gala you were hosting at the gallery, and found testosterone in his fridge and a binder on the couch, you knew these were transmasculine items, thanks to your work to be a better parent to Rock. But you assumed Hobbes was *dating* a trans guy, and hiding his new man from you and Carrie because he was afraid that you'd think he'd gone "back to straight" and invalidate his new and expansive understanding of his sexuality.

What a relief that not only was Hobbes okay, but that you would now be able to infodump to Carrie about the universally agreed-upon differences in implications that the terms bisexual and pansexual hold regarding attraction to trans people, which you strongly believe exist as the result of overzealous workplace ally training! It brings me no joy to say it, Charlotte, but the joy of infodumping clouded your judgement, and while that doesn't make you a bad person, it did delay your finding out about this for a good six weeks.

**When did he realise he was a man?**

The road to transness runs through Gender Non-Conformity Land, a magical place where many of us think only gay people may run free, loving and being loved for whoever they turn out to be. And who can blame this hypothetical person for thinking only gay people can get fucky with gender and still be desired, when their dating pool is the famously open-minded cohort of '90s New York lawyers, finance bros, and property developers (oh my!).

Of course, gay women like women, and Hobbes was no lesbian. (Though not for lack of trying, if the person trying considers the core traits of lesbians to be having short hair and wearing a tie, with the desire or even tolerance to, say, kiss women being besides the point.) So Hobbes, like all horny transfags, was cursed with the seeming paradox of transition: he could either develop attraction to women, who could love him for his masculinity, and be a man, *or* have sex with men, which is what women do, and not be a man. And he was not about to give up boy cock.

If only there was another way!!

Thankfully, this heterosexual Saw trap of the mind was finally broken in season 4 episode 14, when Hobbes had to pee in the gay bar with no ladies' room and saw that guy from work and was like "I had no idea [that you were gay]" and the guy was like, "I had no idea you were a gay man either!" and Hobbes stammered because for the first time in his life he thought, "Oh shit, I can be that?"

And now he is. Because you can't be what you can't pee.

**How does he have sex? Does he do anal now? Because he's gay?**

Obviously, Hobbes has devastating haemorrhoids from being himself for his whole life. Nothing is going in and out and back in and back out and back in there. Taking a more circuitous route to pleasure is fine by Hobbes though, because he's more of a sub4sub edging guy anyway.

**He's a what?**

He wants someone else to be in control, but he's Hobbes, so good luck to anyone trying to tell him what to do. The result is that the kind of sex he wants is desperate, impulsive, messy—both parties surrendering to desire with no one to hold the reins.

He wants a guy to usher him to the bathroom and order him to put his hands on the wall and bend over, pants down. Hobbes will do as he's told, hard as hell because he's finally not the guy in control and really, he never wanted to be. He'll realise he's been holding his breath when he lets out a strangled moan—suddenly stifled by one of his lover's hands as the other slides up and down the length of his t-dick, which this position fully exposes.

His lover is rutting into his pert ass now, getting sloppier as his own cock strains with need in his jeans, and Hobbes feels himself getting close—but so does his lover. Suddenly, he turns Hobbes around, their lips colliding hard, saying I want as much of me inside you as possible right now, before Hobbes drops down, drooling for what he really wants to wrap his lips around. His hands fumble with his lover's belt and fly until he hears that delicious slide of leather, creak of metal loosening its teeth. Hobbes reaches between his lover's legs to fuck his wet hole as his eager mouth parts to swallow that swollen cock—

**Is that how Anthony found out about Hobbes' transition, because he accidentally opened a toilet door right into Hobbes' head, giving him a concussion, because he was on his knees sucking cock in the stall?**
Yes.

**Is it homophobic if the porn made me uncomfortable?**
Absolutely.

**Okay. Well, am I crazy, or would Hobbes and Anthony make a cute couple?**
Don't even think about it, Carrie.

ARIANA MARTINEZ

# Messaging My Motherboard

| Instant Messaging |
| --- |
| **Gaby73:** Hola mi bebe<br>**NotZeroZeroOne:** Hola Mami como estas?<br>**Gaby73:** Bien, watching Sex and the City<br>**NotZeroZeroOne:** Nice, which episode?<br>**Gaby73:** One I've never seen before<br>**NotZeroZeroOne:** Omg, you say that every time! What's the plot?<br>**Gaby73:** Carrie's computer breaks, Miranda's Mami dies, Samantha can't . . . enjoy sex lol<br>**NotZeroZeroOne:** Lol such an unserious show what the f*ck is that combo<br>**Gaby73:** Jajajaja your Papi walked in during Samantha's sex stuff, shook his head, and walked out<br>**NotZeroZeroOne:** Of course he did. I can't believe he ever confused Samantha con Miranda! |

**Gaby73:** Que??

**NotZeroZeroOne:** Remember you told me you wanted to name me Miranda, and he said no because she was the "slut" from Sex and the City

**Gaby73:** LOL siiii. But you know how your Papi is. He says it's stupid and makes fun of me for watching it, but when he comes to bed, he watches a little with me. I just liked the name Miranda!

**NotZeroZeroOne:** I still like it! Plus, she's my favorite. Well, sometimes. I think I'm the most like her

**Gaby73:** Really?

**NotZeroZeroOne:** Oh yeah, work-driven, don't really want kids, cynical

**Gaby73:** Aha, I see it jaja. My favorite is Samantha

**NotZeroZeroOne:** Que??? I figured yours would be Charlotte

**Gaby73:** Charlotte is soo judgmental

**NotZeroZeroOne:** Like you aren't?!

**Gaby73:** Samantha does what she wants. I like that about her. I also like Carrie's style but she's annoying

**NotZeroZeroOne:** She's the worst, but I kind of get what she's going through here

**Gaby73:** Como?

**NotZeroZeroOne:** You know how some things can be an extension of your body? For you, it's your phone because you're always on it

Send

Instant Messaging

**Gaby73:** I have to work, mi linda. Running a business is not easy

**NotZeroZeroOne:** I know. I always loved watching you work when I was a kid. Even before you started the company with Papi, I loved visiting you at Motorola and seeing your cubicle. Plus, you had a bunch of extra phones, which meant I could have a new one every week LOL

**Gaby73:** Ah, I loved that job. Having my own business is different. There's always more work to do. It's exhausting

**Gaby73:** That's why I like watching this show. It lets me disconnect from all the noise of work and just laugh

**NotZeroZeroOne:** You deserve that!

**NotZeroZeroOne:** So yeah, Carrie is crazy, but for people like you and me, our computer breaking can feel like the whole world is falling apart

**Gaby73:** Do you remember the first laptop I got for you? The little red one?

**NotZeroZeroOne:** Omg si! When Tia moved in with us, I thought my cousin's little pink one was the cutest thing ever. Then you got me my own for Christmas :')

**Gaby73:** You were maybe ten? I got my first computer the year you were born

**Gaby73:** Your Papi gave me his old one. It was so big and heavy, but I had it for a long time! It got very slow after a while, but we kept it around

**NotZeroZeroOne:** Oh yeah, that's what I used before you got me my own!
**NotZeroZeroOne:** I'll never forget how slow it got. It was responsible for one of the most embarrassing moments of my childhood
**Gaby73:** Que???
**NotZeroZeroOne:** Lol nothing
**Gaby73:** Oye, tell me!
**Gaby73:** ????

*NotZeroZeroOne is typing . . .*

**I was 10, curious, on websites with sex ads, and clicked everything. Then it crashed, and you saw all of it, and had me write "I'm sorry, God" over and over in a notebook lol**

Send

Instant Messaging

**NotZeroZeroOne:** You know what, let's just drop it LOL

**NotZeroZeroOne:** So, Sex and the City helps you relax?

**Gaby73:** Claro, when your dad and I get home from the office, I go to my room to watch it, and he watches his loud, guns, zombie stuff in the living room. It's really annoying. I can't stand those shows! Tan vulgar. Why would I wanna come home and watch that? Then, at night, he has the craziest dreams! Yelling, kicking around like he's some superhero!

**NotZeroZeroOne:** You gotta admit that's pretty cool

**Gaby73:** You don't have to share a bed with him! I can't sleep!!!!

**NotZeroZeroOne:** Lol both of your tastes in media are so "Men are from Mars, women are from Venus." At least you both like sex in your shows LOL

**Gaby73:** Eh

**NotZeroZeroOne:** Omg, how Samantha is your favorite?? You're not very sexual

**Gaby73:** That's true lol

**NotZeroZeroOne:** That's another way our house is so gendered. Your son is just like your husband (sluts) and I'm like you, more or less

**Gaby73:** More or less?

**NotZeroZeroOne:** Like, I'm also not super sexually adventurous, but I'm not a "woman," so that kinda complicates the picture :p

**Gaby73:** No entiendo
**NotZeroZeroOne:** I don't really know how to explain it
**Gaby73:** Try
**Gaby73:** Please?
**NotZeroZeroOne:** I don't feel strongly about being born a woman
**Gaby73:** I'm not really the biggest girly-girl, either
**NotZeroZeroOne:** It's more than that. I really don't know how to explain it.
**Gaby73:** Keep going
**NotZeroZeroOne:** You know how I was just saying Papi is very masculine. His "sex" at birth is male because of his anatomy. But then, socially, he was raised to inhabit what society thinks being a man should be. You were born a "female," but then socially, you were taught to be emotional, nurturing, to think "pretty" looks a certain way
**NotZeroZeroOne:** Plenty of women defy this "binary" way of viewing gender. For a while, I thought I was that kind of woman, like you.
**NotZeroZeroOne:** That I didn't fit into this box of femininity. But then, my feelings went beyond that. I realized I didn't really buy into this whole gender thing altogether. If all those things are taught to us, then I get to decide how much I internalize that, and

Send

Instant Messaging

I don't anymore. I realized this when I had my first girlfriend. I didn't feel like a girl dating another girl. When I look in the mirror, I don't see a beautiful "woman" I just see me. It's liberating to see myself as more than what the world teaches me to be

**NotZeroZeroOne:** Me entiendes?

**NotZeroZeroOne:** I'm sorry, I just shouldn't have said anything

**Gaby73:** I kind of get it. But not fully

**Gaby73:** Are you still my daughter?

**NotZeroZeroOne:** Yeah. I guess. When I discovered I was nonbinary, I told myself I was going to use "she/they" pronouns because of the family. I knew nobody would understand or make an effort. But then I dropped "she," and I thought I could handle it. But then questions like that just make me feel like what I'm doing isn't worth the trouble. Why call myself something nobody else sees unless I make it clear to them?

**Gaby73:** I'm sorry

**Gaby73:** Did I teach you what it means to be a woman in a way that was bad?

**NotZeroZeroOne:** Of course not

**Gaby73:** Are you sure?

**NotZeroZeroOne:** Remember in the episode, Miranda has to buy a new bra for her mom's funeral and she breaks down? I think my relationship with my breasts was the only nerve that got hit by the

family. You and the other women were always poking them and talking about their size when I just wanted to pretend they didn't exist
**Gaby73:** Yeah, I remember. We meant it as a compliment. Naturally large breasts are a gift
**Gaby73:** Do you think it was bad that I got a boob job?
**NotZeroZeroOne:** No, I get why you did it, but I'm happy you removed them when they began to affect your health
**Gaby73:** Me too. But now I look like a little boy lol
**NotZeroZeroOne:** See I hate that! You feel less like a woman just because you don't have large breasts. That's not fair to you, you're gorgeous
**Gaby73:** Aye, gracias
**NotZeroZeroOne:** You showed me that being a woman meant being hard-working, putting your heart into what you love, making people meals not because you're a servant but because you want them to be full and taken care of. Basic gender roles are pretty relevant in our home, but not in some evil way. You have never been weak or docile. You inspire me.
**NotZeroZeroOne:** I'm not, not a woman because of anything you did wrong
**Gaby73:** Thank you. I'm sorry I don't completely understand how you feel

Send

Instant Messaging

**NotZeroZeroOne:** Thanks for trying.
**Gaby73:** It feels silly to talk about a t.v. show now
**NotZeroZeroOne:** It's a little silly, but in a way that's special. That episode is a solid encapsulation of the frustrating aspects of the show but its possibilities for endearment. Miranda grieves. Samantha cries. Charlotte nurtures. Carrie is dreadful but finds a way to connect it all and advocate for growth. And now we know each other better because of it
**Gaby73:** Te amo mucho mi bebe
**NotZeroZeroOne:** I love you too Mami
**Gaby73:** The second movie is really terrible though, I hate it

Send

DANI JANAE

# Dining In:

## *Sex and the City*'s Portrayal of Dykes

*Sex and the City* is still lauded as groundbreaking television for its depictions of women's sexuality. It unabashedly approaches sex and desire in a way that most shows didn't at the time, especially not with regards to women in their thirties. But while *SATC* celebrates its heroines' hetero dalliances, its perfunctory explorations of queerness fall short.

The show did feature white gay men from the start, but in highly stereotyped ways: *SATC*'s gay guys are effeminate, bitchy, and always ready with a devastating quip about someone's looks or status. Meanwhile, we barely see lesbians in season 1, and when they finally arrive en masse in S2E6, I find their portrayal, well, miserable.

At an opening for lesbian artist Yael, Charlotte is introduced to a group of dykes with great shoes and flawlessly "invisible" makeup. Led by Eileen (Tamara Tunie) in a strong-shouldered gray suit, the power lesbians are chic and very, very rich. When Eileen and her ex Lydia return to pick up the painting they purchased, they invite Charlotte to a "girl bar" called G-Spot. After an evening of drinks, dancing, and sapphic French-fusion cuisine, Charlotte begins to question why she values relationships with men more than those with women.

In this episode, Charlotte's storyline comes to a close with a party at one of the power dyke's mansions. The group thinks that Charlotte is gay and interested in Lydia. When questioned, Charlotte admits that she is "sexually" straight, but adds that she "connects to the female spirit." Patty (Jodi Long) delivers a scathing rebuke: "That's all very nice, but if you're not going to eat pussy, you're not a dyke."

I'm fully aware that this was the '90s, and that sexual politics were not where they are now, but I couldn't help but wonder, what the fuck? Yes it's a funny line, but underneath it is a very rigid, very reformed idea of what a lesbian is. If eating pussy makes you a dyke, then what does that mean for pillow princesses? What does that mean for touch-me-nots? What does it mean for dykes without pussies? The power lesbians may be rich and fashionable and artsy, but they also are bound to rigid definitions of lesbianism.

Now, none of the lesbians I personally know are millionaires with mansions and disposable income galore, and maybe that's what makes us less defined by what makes or breaks a lesbian. Climbing the social and economic ranks definitely changes a person. It's not that the struggle makes you more pure, but that being rich and powerful corrupts you. You become more willing to conform to heteronormative ideals of what sex and relationships should look like. While it may sound harsh, we've seen it time and time again: gay celebrities and elites that turn into conservatives when it's time to stand for something.

But while it's possible that the showrunners were making some kind of social commentary about the corrupting power of wealth, it's more likely that they just don't understand dykes. After all, *SATC* also bumbles its attempts at broaching topics like race and addiction. Perhaps homosexuality is just another fumbled talking point—one that the show routinely struggles to tackle.

In S1E3, for instance, Miranda gets set up by her colleagues at the law firm. When she arrives at the softball game where she is supposed to meet this potential beau, she's mortified to find out that Syd, her date, is . . . a woman! Instead of being upfront with her date, Miranda is cold; she confronts the person that set her up, and later confesses to Syd that she's not gay. The two go on to play a great game of softball and even hug when their firm wins.

As a viewer, you might think that's where the story ends, but not quite. A senior partner at her firm presents Miranda with an opportunity to climb the ranks, but only if she and Syd present as a couple. So Miranda uses Syd as a pawn in her scheme to make partner. Syd agrees to this, so I can't totally place all the blame on Miranda, but it is in fact quite miserable to play the girlfriend of someone you just met in order for that person to get a raise.

Of course, when it comes down to it, Miranda can't even pretend to be a lesbian—it's too awkward for her. She confesses to her boss that the whole thing was a ploy; then, on the elevator ride down, feeling alone and desperate, she kisses Syd, glumly concluding that she is "definitely straight."

Miranda does eventually, sort of, come out in *And Just Like That . . .* , but even then, she seems to have a narrow idea of what a lesbian or queer woman is. Yes, she's just at the start of her journey, but it's all the more complicated by the fact that she doesn't know there are many representations of queerness that could fit her. Now, I've been out since I was 12 and building queer community since then, so maybe this comes off as judgmental, but I think Miranda's foray into queerness is all the more clumsy because she has no queer women in her life to help usher her into the world.

Miranda falls into a common trap among queer women: making your first queer relationship your entire world. Hell, she leaves her husband of 20 years, turns down a dream internship, and moves temporarily to Los Angeles, all for a nonbinary podcaster. Everything she is learning about herself and her queerness is through the lens of *does Che like this? Is this appealing to Che? Will this help me maintain my relationship with Che?* She never really stops to ask herself what she wants and needs.

Miranda does explore herself more after her breakup with Che, as she meets and romances an audiobook narrator named Ameilia, but the woman is a walking negative lesbian stereotype and I hated watching them interact. Luckily, Miranda eventually comes to her senses and flees Amelia's cat litter-strewn apartment. Maybe season 3 Miranda will have better luck?

Of course, I would be remiss if I didn't include Samantha's brief foray into lesbianism. In S4E3, Samantha begins a relationship with artist Maria Reyes. Her friends are shocked that she's in a relationship with *anyone*, gay or otherwise; but, overall, this storyline is treated like another of Samantha's frivolous sexual exploits, rather than as a genuine exploration of sexuality.

The relationship starts with sex that seems to excite and challenge Samantha, but like many lesbian relationships portrayed in media, the sex dwindles and the endless "processing" begins. While Samantha seems hellbent on keeping things casual, Maria repeatedly pushes to escalate their partnership, forcing a reluctant Samantha to tell her friends about their relationship. It's a well-trodden stereotype that lesbians are overly committal, severely monogamous, and boring. *Sex and the City* plays right into this stereotype by casting Maria as pushy and jealous.

I've known all kinds of dykes in my life: monogamous, polyamorous, reserved, intense, emotional, detached. We come in all shapes and flavors, and the show really fails to depict that variety. The writers can dream up an endless parade of straight-white-guy love interests, but we can't even get one depiction of a lesbian that doesn't suck?

Of course, one could argue that all of *SATC*'s main characters kind of suck, too. Carrie is delusional, Charlotte is obsessed with conforming, Miranda is a hard-ass, and Samantha is flighty. But these women also get the opportunity to be multi-faceted: they are successful businesswomen, stylish socialites, and loyal friends. Meanwhile, the lesbians in this show are very one-note, or not even a note at all.

What I love about the dykes in my life is that we don't seek to conform to definitions of lesbianism that stifle us. Some of us are married with kids and some of us are throwing sex parties. (Some of us are doing both!) We're dykes whether or not we eat pussy or have our pussies eaten, or whatever else happens in the bedroom. Just like Carrie and her friends, we live the lives that we want, messy and all. Too bad we'll never see that on *SATC*.

KIT MILLS

# Unwelcome to the Dollhouse

ahem

hello

i'm mary, queen of scots.

UM... HELLO? I'M STANFORD BLATCH.
...TALENT AGENT.
you know, my second husband was a homosexual too.
EXCUSE ME?

oh, yes! well, likely bisexual. of course, historical understandings of queerness are complicated and nuanced, and it's difficult to say how lord darnley would have defined his sexuality had terms like "straight" or "gay" existed in the 16th century.
though a lot of his contemporaries basically called him a nancy boy.

but whatever. regardless of the specifics of identity, he **definitely** murdered his ex-boyfriend right in front of me!
it was all **very** dramatic and did **not** help my career.
WOW, UH, THAT SOUNDS REALLY TOUGH BUT I'M **NOT** REALLY IN THE MOOD FOR A HISTORY LESSON...
but honestly that was the **least** of our issues as a couple.
there was all the drinking-
EXCUSE ME-
and the scheming to claim the english throne for himself
HEY!
and then my own **cousin** had me beheaded-
LADY!!
WITH ALL DUE RESPECT TO A FELLOW QUEEN, I'M TRYING TO GET **LAID** HERE! I'VE HAD ENOUGH OF PLAYING THERAPIST TO ROMANTICALLY-TORTURED STRAIGHT WOMEN AND I AM OFFICIALLY OFF THE CLOCK! I'M ONLY HERE BECAUSE MY USUAL FAG HAG MADE A BET WITH ME SO SHE'D HAVE AN EXCUSE TO QUIT SMOKING.
I BET SHE'S HAVING A CIG RIGHT NOW
DON'T TALK TO HER LIKE THAT
SHE'S BEEN THROUGH A LOT

I THINK YOU SHOULD GO.
FINE. I GUESS I'M NOT ENOUGH OF A QUEEN TO DATE A QUEEN WHO COLLECTS QUEENS AFTER ALL.
NO
into thy hands, o lord, i commend my spirit.
again.
SOUNDS LIKE YOUR DATE WAS A ROYAL FUCK-UP
I JUST WISH I'D GOTTEN HEAD BEFORE SHE LOST HER HEAD.
KM 2024

# MONKED;

## or, Sex and the Monastery

Stanford Blatch got Monked. That is to say, when actor Willie Garson died, the writers of *And Just Like That . . .* wrote his character out of the show by sending him to Japan to spend the rest of his life as a Shinto monk. When Carrie broke the news to Blatch's in-show husband, Anthony Marantino, he responded with an ineffectual, "Good for him." The immediate equanimity, closure, and lack of curiosity around this little plot twist led my friends and I to pause the show on the television and evaluate ourselves for neurological irregularities. Anthony, you're just . . . not going to follow up? Liza Minnelli sang at your wedding. You're not going to at least check if you have airline points to go find him?

The task of writing out a character due to the actor's death is a difficult and delicate challenge, and I don't envy it. This particular scene, however, feels so out of the realm of human experience that I assume it was penned by gerbils; creatures close enough to observe our behavior but not enough to get it right.

My best friend and I adopted the phrase "getting Monked" to describe this kind of no-fault ghosting. Oh, what happened to that person you matched with? *They got Monked.* If you're ditching your date, you Monked 'em. Leaving your spouse and quitting your kids for enlightenment's sake? You Monked, baby. We imagined future seasons of the show as a kind of Battle Royale for the rest of the characters: The moment anyone ran out of narrative potential, or the second an actor tried to renegotiate a contract, the gerbils would excuse them to a far-flung monastery for the rest of their days—and everyone else had to be *so* happy for them. Each beloved character would slowly defect one by one to a life of reflection in a holy place, until there was no Sex, just an anonymous City.

Here is the proposed order for the rest of the characters to get Monked, one that the cowards at the helm of the show would not be brave enough to admit is the correct way to finish out this tepid, garish affair:

**Che Diaz** gets Monked next, not because it makes sense for the character but because we already know the character isn't returning, and there is no use in trying to blah-blah a thing about LA. The rest of the podcast pals try to persuade Che to come back to showbiz, and in the process, get Monked themselves, which is mentioned offhand at girls' brunch.

The mostly white writers seem to be utterly unable to craft a credible storyline for **Dr. Nya Wallace**, and we know that actress Karen Pittman is leaving the show, so let's drag this Monking out by having her go on academic sabbatical, get taken in by a niche spiritual group, and decide to quit the rat race.

Because the gerbils were not brave enough to simply let the unsinkable **Samantha Jones** die of cancer with dignity, I humbly suggest that she be Monked instead. Give her a beautiful Monking. Let the postscript be that she slowly turned her spiritual community into a sex cult, but a fun one. Friar Fuck, after all. And then everyone, please leave her alone. **Smith** quietly Monks after, and it's barely mentioned.

**Aidan Shaw** Monks *hard*. He gets back in touch with Carrie to tell her that after the intensity of taking care of his troubled son, he needs to reconnect with himself, and would she be willing to extend her period of waiting around for him by another decade or two? And that throws her into an existential arc that will pay off later, be patient. **Steve** Monks along with him, why not.

The bread industry tanks. **Anthony** gets Monked.

**Seema** gets Monked and gives up her oh-so-fabulous lifestyle with a level of asceticism that's not quite credible due to the character's firm materialistic nature, and the show underscores the scene with music that's culturally insensitive. That's not to say that this is my preference; I'm just trying to keep things realistic with the show's track record.

**Lisa Todd Wexley** Monks next, because it's a thing in her well-heeled set, and actually probably because the whole miscarriage plotline was so poorly handled.

**Rock** Monks. Rock has been sick of the silver spoon lifestyle they have led thus far and takes that yearning to the ultimate conclusion, dedicating their life to deeper meaning. They regret this choice two weeks in when they realize how bland the food is, and how there's nothing to do but pray. But they are stubborn, so they remain, to avoid the look on their parents' faces.

Moved by this, **Charlotte** gets Monked a few episodes later. She fundamentally misunderstands her role as parent and ally, and lets that take her all the way to a monastery in Portugal, because it's covered in beautiful art. She gets used to flats, tends to the garden, and stops thinking about her life before.

There is a brief and ill-advised spinoff show featuring **Harry Goldenblatt** called *Harry in a Hurry*, about his search for a new wife, but three episodes in he is Monked, and the last 20 minutes of the episode is a contemplative, unbroken shot of Madison Square Fountain.

Word goes round that **Jack Berger** has Monked, and Carrie intones the customary, "Good for him." He escapes because the self-awareness and interiority was killing him, but he writes a best-selling memoir about it.

**Miranda** Monks after checking on her oldest friend. She leaves with the type-A grace reminiscent of her days as a corporate lawyer, the days before she was a sloppy drunk who orgasmed from a single finger in the kitchen while Carrie pissed in a bottle next door. She leaves no box unchecked, no untidy bill or unread email. Miranda is done with capitalism, having felt so deeply harmed by a life of comp-het, of feminism curled into the form patriarchy demanded of her, of the scorn directed at her for aging, for not knowing, for still learning. She opens.

The City is full of ghosts. The diner is quiet. The streets are empty, and **Carrie**'s whole life feels like the day after Christmas in New York, before things fill up and start again. She moves in the motions of her former self, walking through places she once knew and now finds uncanny and unfamiliar. She walks until concrete breaks into grass, until the light of the sky is blocked by no building, until she feels her lungs burning with effort and good, clean air.

Carrie ditches her shoes. She walks until the idea of a Carrie splits apart, atomizes as if she sprang forth through a perfume nozzle, out of the bottleneck of a city and into the atmosphere, her essence sizzling intangible and incorporated into every other thing in the wild world. Her breath is a prayer. Her feet are an abbey. There are no end credits, only the tangled loops of god and spring.

JAS BROWN

# Which *SATC* Quote Is Your Queer Breakup Style?

If the queers and *SATC* girlies can agree on one thing, it's the importance of knowing when to walk away. As much fun as it is to flirt with someone new, sometimes you need to drop the dead weight to get to your perfect U-Haul or dream polycule. Despite their mostly straight tendencies, Carrie, Sam, Char, and Miranda may have some hot tips for your next breakup.

For each question, note which answer sounds most like you. Remember: this is just for funsies, so don't take it too seriously.

## 1. You're going out tonight. What are you wearing?

✦) the all-black outfit you wear every night—it's simple and gets the job done

♣) something flirty, with a wistful pink blush on your cheeks and butterfly clips in your hair

▶) the chunkiest boots you own—you look hot, and they're great for dancing

⊙) something you coordinated with your friend group

◕) whatever you were wearing last night because you haven't been home in a few days

**2. You lock eyes with a cutie at the local lesbian bar and give them a wink. What were you in the middle of doing?**

♣) fantasizing with your friends about your dream date

✦) working the room to get over your recent breakup—why process your feelings when you could just kiss someone else?

⊙) having a passionate heart-to-heart with your friend about all the reasons you love each other

◕) flirting with the person you're currently on a date with—it's always good to have a backup in case this date doesn't work out

▶) singing "Red Wine Supernova" for karaoke night—everyone's eyes are on you and you love it!

**3. You and the cutie swap numbers and they text you "Hi!" the next day. What's your response?**

✦) "hi"

▶) "sorry, just getting this now, I was out of town for a few days"

◕) “who’s this?”

⊙) “I was just thinking about you, how are you?”

♣) “hiiiiii 💘 🦋 wow feeling exhausted from that full moon last night hbu?”

## 4. You ask them out on a first date. What’s your plan?

⊙) fancy dinner—you need to see if they are relationship material

♣) picnic on the beach—you want to show off your cute picnic outfit and charcuterie skills

✦) coffee date—the perfect place to ask them questions and learn more about them

▶) invite them to a party you’re already going to—keeps things fun and low-pressure

◕) you forgot to plan something so you invite them over to your place last minute

## 5. You’ve been going out for a while but things have felt off lately. What’s wrong?

◕) you’ve broken up and gotten back together several times, but it’s for different reasons each time—maybe this time it will stick?

♣) they aren’t putting in enough effort to woo you

✦) you’re feeling smothered but don’t know how to tell them

▶) you've been really busy and haven't had much time to spend with them

⊙) you feel like you aren't making much progress in couples therapy

## 6. It's not working out and it's time to break up. What's your move?

⊙) schedule a meeting to figure out a shared custody arrangement for your cat

▶) ask them to meet you for coffee near your gym, so you can at least get a workout in afterwards

♣) ask them to meet at the location of your first date and show up with flowers—who said breakups can't be cinematic?

◕) after spending the night at their place, text them a shrug emoji and question mark on your way out

✦) slowly stop responding to their texts—maybe they will get the hint when they see you with someone else?

## Results

Add up how many times you selected each symbol to find your breakup quote.

### If you selected mostly ✦:

**"You know what used to make me feel better? Cookies."**
**—Miranda**, after wolfing down the entirety of a giant "I love you" cookie from her boyfriend rather than saying it back.

In matters of the heart, you would rather lead with your head and leave the messy feelings for another day. Your breakups are just a problem to be solved, but when you realize you can't logic your way out of an emotional breakdown, you're often left feeling overwhelmed. Be sure to balance your analytical side with a healthy dose of intuition now and then, and maybe stop rolling your eyes when your friend offers you a tarot reading.

### If you selected mostly ♣:

**"I am someone who is looking for love. Real love. Ridiculous, inconvenient, consuming, can't-live-without-each-other love."**
**—Carrie**, after following Mikhail Baryshnikov to Paris and getting disappointed when he was too busy to constantly adore her.

You have big dreams for love and aren't afraid to pursue them at all costs. Dating you can be intense, dreamy, and romantic, but you have a tendency to cut things off once the glitter fades. Beware of setting your standards higher than any human can feasibly reach; even in the most passionate relationships, you sometimes need to deal with bad breath.

### If you selected mostly ▶:

> **"I love you too . . . but I love me more."**
> —**Samantha**, after deciding that she can no longer dedicate her life to catching her cheating boyfriend in the act (even if he does have a perfect dick).

You are the main character and aren't afraid to ask for what you want and need. Your own interests are a priority, and you aren't afraid to move on if your dates can't keep up. In your quest for independence, remember to keep your heart open to love—sometimes we all need to compromise a bit.

### If you selected mostly ⊙:

> **"And I don't think I should have to give that up."**
> —**Charlotte**, who gave her marriage her all, but wanted a baby and wasn't about to let post-*Twin Peaks*, pre-*Brat*-era Kyle MacLachlan stand in her way.

You are committed to your loved ones and aren't afraid of working hard and compromising to stay together. Sometimes this will lead you to stay in relationships long after their expiration date and only call it quits once you're emotionally burned out. Be sure to attend to your own needs, too, and remember who you are outside of your relationships.

### If you selected mostly ◕:

> **"I'm sorry. I can't. Don't hate me."**
>
> **—Berger to Carrie**, unceremoniously, on a Post-it note.

Let's be honest: you're messy. You don't break up with people as much as you make them question whether you were even dating in the first place. We love embracing the fun of a little chaos, but consider being more upfront with your dates now and then (and don't break up with your long-term partner by text).

MONTREAL BENESCH & COOPER BEDIN

# Carrie's Fables;

## or, How I Learned to Stop Misgendering and Love Trans People

*And Just Like That . . .* feels in many ways like an attempt to atone for the sins of *Sex and the City*. In the opening episode, Miranda arrives at her law class and refers to a blue-haired fellow student with he/him pronouns. The student immediately replies, "Someone's quick with the pronouns," signaling to the audience that the writers are hip to the whole pronouns thing, and that Miranda is going to learn, as they did, how to be woke about trans people. This scene screams, *we're sorry that the only time trans people appeared on the original series was when Samantha berated and harassed Black trans sex workers.*

The swift scolding of Miranda by the blue-haired/pronouns'd student is emblematic of the show's larger approach to morality. Throughout the show, problems such as body dysmorphia or alcoholism are assigned to characters seemingly at random, and each issue is resolved quickly and tidily. Charlotte feels insecure about her tummy until she sees one fat person with an exposed midriff; Miranda is briefly in denial about her alcoholism, but joins AA the instant she admits she has a problem. And just like that . . . everything's fixed!

We use the phrase "Carrie's Fables" to describe the moral frame by which the show operates. In the world of *And Just Like That . . .*, nearly any problem can be assigned to any person at any time, rather than being situated in the identity and experience of a character. This strategy allows the audience to imagine themselves in any character's shoes—even the (gasp!) "diverse" characters. Each character gets one season-long Big Problem; in the meantime, they clear many smaller hurdles, each with its own lesson. Furthermore, entire characters are clearly written with the purpose of teaching the audience how to be members of polite society. This is especially apparent in the show's handling of trans characters—in watching the other characters learn their way around Che, the cisgenders in the audience learn the right way to be normal about trans people.

Che Diaz, standup comic and "queer, nonbinary, Mexican-Irish diva representing everyone else outside these two boring genders," feels like attempted reparations for the representational crimes of *Sex and the City*. Their confidence and sexual success is meant to counter media depictions of trans folks as tragic and lonely. This isn't speculation; Che tells us so the first time we see them perform comedy:

> Every time we are represented in mainstream media . . . there's just one sad, nonbinary character . . . but I have got news for those motherfuckers: I'm not always sad! I laugh all the fucking time! And I'm not always alone!

It is unclear what any of this is doing in a stand-up comedy set.

Perhaps unsurprisingly, the first season's attempt at nonbinary representation was not received well by audiences. "Che Diaz is gonna get gay rights taken away from us," playwright Matthew K. Begbie joked on Twitter. As *Daily Beast* writer Kevin Fallon put it, "There is no exaggerating how insufferable this character is. To call them unwatchable is not hyperbole. 'Cringing' is not a strong enough verb to describe what the body reflexively does when they are on screen, like a physical defense mechanism."

In the same way that Che's presence initially apologized for *Sex and the City*, Che's storyline in the second season of *And Just Like That . . .* apologized for the first. This apology came in the form of character depth, i.e., body dysmorphia. There are many narrative tools that could be used to add depth to a character, and it's striking that the writers of the show again and again choose the avenue of structural pain.

Despite the obvious relationship between body image issues and gender dysphoria, throughout Che's struggles with their weight, their embodied gender experience is never brought up. This is because of the "Carrie's Fables" approach to morality: body dysmorphia was an issue the writers wished to make a statement about, and so they threw a dart at a board and picked Che as the vehicle for their story. It's a coincidence, not a narrative choice, that Che is both the only focal trans adult and assigned to deal with internalized fatphobia. An intersectional critique about gender, fatness, and the body (god forbid race!) would be too narrow for the audience to relate to, and too structurally real to be overcome. Instead, in this world, all it takes is a little validation from Miranda, and just like that . . . Che's body dysmorphia is gone, never to be an issue again.

The bigger audience lesson that has been assigned to Che is The Importance of Nonbinary Representation. This message is *so* important that it is allowed to be Che's season-long Big Problem. Their TV show, *Che Pasa*, doesn't get picked up because queer people didn't feel represented by it; in a focus group for *Che Pasa*, one nonbinary attendee said:

> The whole Che character was like a walking Boomer joke that felt so fake to me. Just some phony, sanitized, performative, cheesy-ass, dad joke, bullshit version of what the nonbinary experience is. It sucked.

In this moment, it feels as though the writers are grabbing us by the shoulders, looking us in the eyes, and saying, *we're sorry we didn't do a good job representing the Nonbinary Experience in season 1. However, we've learned from our mistakes, and are going to do better. We must do better, because the state of Nonbinary Representation on television is so dire. But, we're still going to cancel* Che Pasa.

After moping for several episodes about their failed pilot, Che decides to revisit their old standup routines. First, they watch a set they performed in S1E3 about nonbinary representation. Then, they click over to a video of a set they did 11 years prior—i.e., pretransition. We're given, just for a moment, a window into who Che might have been if they had been on the original run of *Sex and the City*: straight ("Give it up for Jay Mendez! I did. Ugh, he's so hot.") and a woman ("I don't know if other ladies can relate to this . . ."). Younger Che also retroactively plants the seeds for Che's body dysmorphia (which otherwise came from nowhere) as they talk about not eating in order to be more attractive to the men they're trying to date:

> 'I'll have the small dinner salad . . . Cause I'm petite. Hehe. No I am, I am, this is all boob weight. Mm.' And now I've got his full attention.

The juxtaposition of these two comedy routines spoonfeeds the audience Che's entire character arc: from body dysmorphia (but not in a gender dysphoria way!) to the distinct, unrelated problem of being a nonbinary person who is sometimes misgendered (but experiences no structural transphobia!).

Watching their old standup seems to compel Che to debut a set in which they viciously attack Miranda; unbeknownst to them, however, Miranda is in the audience watching. The two fight in the street outside the comedy club, and after Miranda storms off a (clearly nonbinary) audience member comes up to Che and consoles them, flirtily assuring them that they were definitely in the right for publicly defaming their ex. Che eventually makes peace with Miranda, but their last scene in the show is of them making out with their new suitxr.

Che won't be back for season 3. According to an interview in *Variety* with the *AJLT* writers, their arc "had reached a natural conclusion, since their relationship with Miranda had ended." But really, the writers don't need a trans adult character anymore because they've adequately represented the issues trans people face today: social misgendering and a lack of representation in media. The erasure of structural transphobia from trans narratives—despite the show's grappling with many other profound issues—gives cis audience members false assurances about the issues real trans people face in our lives. It felt, at times, like a parody of the queer and trans world in which real people (like us!) live and operate.

*And Just Like That . . .* has taken it upon itself to educate the world. Che constantly gets misgendered, and every time it occurs, the misgendering is met with a correction and clear restatement of their pronouns. Through this, the cis audience learns how to Do Gender Pronouns, while the trans audience wishes we didn't have to do that shit all the time. Che monologues under the guise of doing standup, and the cis audience feels inspired (and in the case of Miranda, aroused) while the trans audience cringes. It's more than a sitcom—it's woke. It's educational. It's . . . "Carrie's Fables."

QUINN BURTON

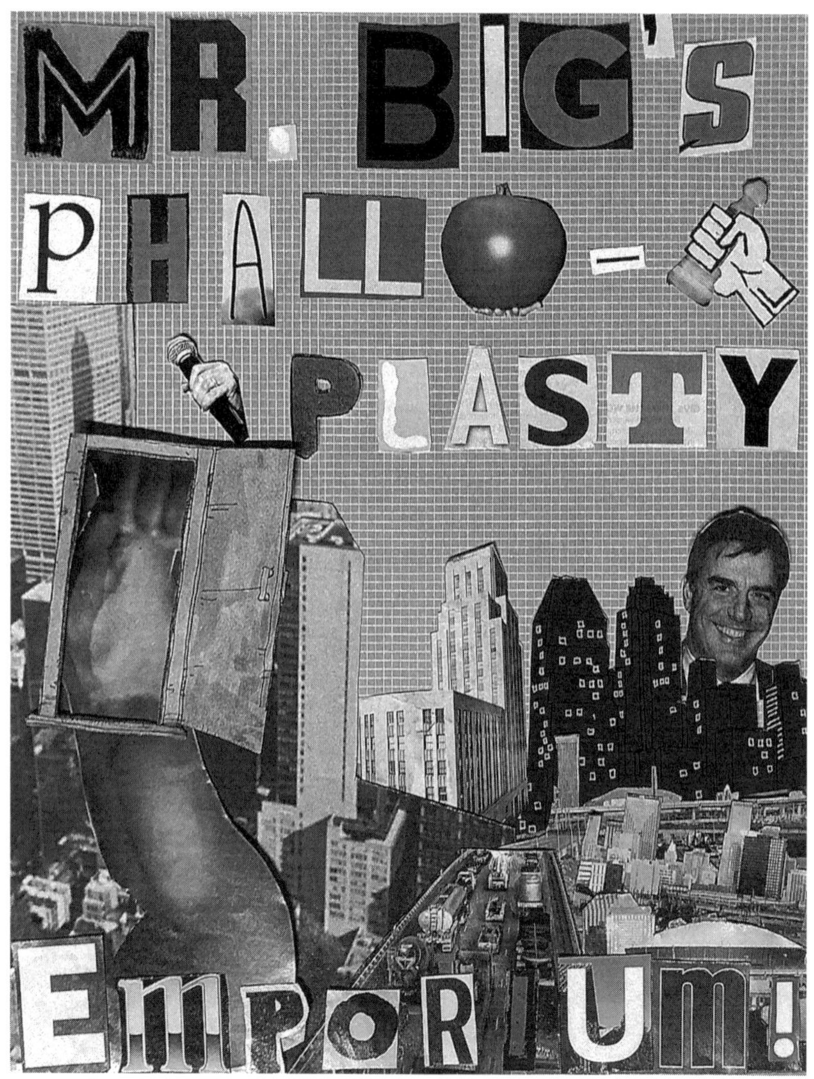

As I drifted off to sleep a few nights ago, the faint recollection of Colby Gordon's exploration of the virtues of phallo in a 2024 *Gender Reveal* episode melded in my head with the knowledge of this forthcoming *SATC* book to produce the phrase "Mr. Big's Phalloplasty Emporium." I repeatedly turned these words over in my mind, but conked out before I could write them down. However, when I awoke the next morning, they were still with me. I took this as a sign that this phrase would be at the center of any submission I produced, and sure enough, here it is—living on in a collage with only the most tenuous of connections to the program. A dream of a better world: a timeline in which transmascs can receive quality phalloplasties free of charge from Carrie's on-again, off-again boyfriend, a world-renowned surgeon whose humility demands that he eschew "Dr." for "Mr."

NINA KATZ

# Critical Condition

## Face to Face with the Other Nina Katz

The aspens were peaking yellow all around as a friend and I hiked along the Jicarita Creek, contemplating what they should change their name to. We hopped over cow pies, stopping to fondle globs of quartz along the trail. "What about Quartz?" I suggested. Not for them.

"It just doesn't feel like me anymore," they said about the name I'd always called them by. We didn't land on anything, and then the question of name-changing turned to me. Did I want to change my name like I'd been changing my body, my pronouns, or the way I dress?

My first name is Nina—a close spelling to "Niña," which literally translates to "little girl" in Spanish. Despite otherwise orienting further from the feminine, I actually like and feel connected to my girl-name and have not (yet) felt a desire to change it.

I like my first name, but I *love* my full name: Nina Katz. It looks neat written down, all balanced with 4 letters each in both first and last. I spent all of elementary-through-grad school doodling it in bubble letters in the margins of my class notes. Camp counselors, teammates, and friends have often referred to me by both first and last name, which has always made me feel not only cool, but known. "Nina Katz!" is how my longtime friend Marina picks up the phone when I call. "It just sounds *so* good," she'll occasionally add.

This sentiment is shared by Samantha Jones and Carrie Bradshaw. In S5E6 of *Sex and the City*, they meet Nina Katz, the character with whom I share a name, and the fictional SNL casting agent with whom Carrie shares an ex: Nina Katz was Aidan's first girlfriend after Carrie. In the episode "Critical Condition," Nina and Carrie run into each other in the bathroom of Stanford's boyfriend's Broadway revue. Nina admits to recognizing Carrie from her column, *then* admits to being the person Aidan dated immediately after Carrie cheated on him with Big. The tryst ended Carrie and Aidan's engagement. Nina Katz was the rebound.

At the bathroom sink, Nina flashes Carrie a damning, all-knowing look, landing Nina the nickname "The Face Girl." Samantha and Carrie refer to Nina by her full name six times in less than a minute of banter, and then four more times before the episode is over. As a character, Nina Katz is a reflection of Carrie's fears about what her ex, and her ex's ex, think of her. "Fuck that fucking face girl," Miranda exclaims at brunch, as Carrie confesses her fixation on Nina Katz. I'm flattered.

My first exposure to *SATC* Nina Katz came in 2008, before I had ever watched the show. I was in ninth-grade Theater A, a class that often turned into *Whose Line Is It Anyway?* marathons on the projector. One day, the teacher called me over just as I swung my hips into my hard plastic seat by the window looking out onto the football field. I stood back up and nervously walked over to her desk, where, on her desktop, she had pulled up the scene on YouTube.

She told me she had been watching reruns of the show the night before, and that she thought of me when this episode came on." You'll see why," she said with a grin. She played the clip as my classmates trickled in, cramming lines they were supposed to have already memorized for our impending Shakespeare activity. But the only lines I could focus on were those coming out of Kim Cattrall and Sarah Jessica Parker's mouths. I knew I would never forget them: "How do you know Nina Katz?" Samantha posits to Carrie. "How do *you* know Nina Katz?" Carrie quips back. "Nina Katz *loves* to talk," says Samantha. "Just like you," my theater teacher cracked at me. Mean, sure, but I hadn't felt this special since before I started high school.

Eventually, I watched the entire show. Since then, every few years, I've watched it again and again. Again and again people ask me, "Have you watched *SATC*?" I'm such a killjoy when I admit I already know about the episode, but share that I'm glad they're so excited, with the reminder that I was born (and named) eight years before it ever aired. But I'll admit that since being introduced to the clip as a 13-year-old, this episode has become my greatest party trick, my go-to fun fact that makes me the star of awkward rounds of icebreaker introductions.

Having the same name as a one-off *SATC* character is also my built-in barometer for the show's cultural relevance. As long as people bring up the Nina Katz episode to me, I can know for sure that *SATC* is still being consumed by the masses. Once, my psychiatrist's administrative assistant asked me if I'd seen the episode while taking my blood pressure. She'd just watched it with her daughter the night before. I was there to get drugs I hoped would help me freak out less about not being a girl.

"I can't change my name," I said to my friend on our hike. "If I did, I wouldn't have the same name as Nina Katz from *SATC* anymore."

I've always worn my name-likeness to the Face Girl as a badge of honor. In fact, if not for Nina Katz (fictional), I question whether I'd still be so attached to my very non-fictional name. My dedication to mainstream culture, to which *SATC* belongs, led me to believe I had to be straight and/or cis, and inhibited me from knowing a sense of gender euphoria. Certainly, *SATC* Nina Katz could be a part of that problem, blocking my path towards realizing a more trans life for myself. If this episode leaves Carrie with a critical condition of worrying about what other people think of her, it's conditioned me to worry about how I think of *myself*. I can't help but wonder: what would I know that I don't know now if I let go of Nina Katz?

# My Beautiful Girlfriend, Samantha Jones

"So, just, chop?" Carrie asks with a laugh, slashing the air in front of her. "Bye bye, boobies?"

"Carrie!" Miranda chides, hitting Carrie's arm with a limp-wristed slap.

"What?" Carrie looks conspiratorial. "She doesn't mind, right?" Miranda and Charlotte eye me like an off-leash dog, their mouths upturned but their eyes unsure. I push a crouton through some Caesar dressing, and Samantha gives my thigh a squeeze under the table.

"*They* may be too polite to say anything," she says, staring daggers at her friends, "but *I* am going to have to insist that you stop being ignorant hags if you don't want me to make a scene at brunch." I avert my eyes and suppress a grin.

"It's really okay, Sam," I begin. "Carrie's a journalist! She's curious!" I force a smile in Carrie's direction. "Right?"

"See, *Sam*!" Carrie beams. "She—or 'they'" (she adds exaggerated air quotes here as she makes eye contact with Samantha) "gets it!"

At the end of brunch, like always, I make a show of pulling my debit card out of my wallet, and, also like always, Sam rolls her eyes and tells me to put it away. In the taxi to her penthouse, after thanking her again for the salad, I tell her, only half joking, that I don't want her to think I'm taking advantage of her generosity.

"Oh please," she says, teasing. "I wish you'd take *more* of my money and let me be a proper Sugar Mommy!" She puts a hand on my waist and lowers her voice, staring straight into my eyes. "And I *really* wish you'd take advantage of me."

Samantha and I have been dating for a few months now, and, though we're not exclusive (she made it clear on our second date that monogamy isn't for her, and I surprised her by agreeing), we're not casual either. When I told her about my surgery, she took off the whole week to help me out, despite my feeble lie that I'd be fine on my own.

The night before, Samantha sleeps over at my place. She smiles when she sees, on my dresser, printed aftercare instructions and a living will.

"What?" I smile back, daring her to tease me. But instead of making a joke, she wraps her arms around my waist from behind, rests her head on my shoulder, and tells me she likes how I worry about everything.

"You're like a little dog, shaking and shivering all the time," she says gently, kissing my neck.

She's not wrong. Later that night, I try to avoid the urge to toss and turn in bed, electric at the thought of the day awaiting me. I think Sam's asleep until she whispers, "Are you excited?" into the nape of my neck.

"Yeah," I say quietly. "And nervous."

"What are you scared of?" she asks as I roll over to face her in the dark. "Well, dying," I begin, and Samantha laughs.

"Oh, honey! Do you know how many surgeries I've had *for fun*? They'll give you some drugs, you'll take a nap, and you'll wake up with a huge weight off your chest!"

"Oh my god . . ." I groan, unable to suppress a laugh.

After a few moments, she asks if there's anything else I'm worried about. "I'm . . ." I struggle to keep the tremor out of my voice. "I guess I'm just worried you'll . . . I don't know. That you'll feel differently about me, maybe. Like, you won't be attracted to me anymore." At this, Samantha moves away from me, so I can see her eyes staring into mine in the moonlight dripping in through the blinds.

"I love *you*," she says solemnly. "And if this makes you *more you*, then how could it do anything but make me love you more?"

She pulls me in close, and I fall asleep sobbing in her soft arms.

The first few days of my recovery are only mildly humiliating. Samantha insists on holding my hand to the bathroom ("Doctor's orders!"), and, when I tell her I don't need help measuring the fluid in my drains, she rolls her eyes.

"Sweetie, I had *cancer*, and, though I may or may not have gone through menopause," (pause for laugh) "if you think I'm a stranger to a little bit of blood, we might need to lower your next dose of Vicodin."

We snuggle on the couch and watch *Ultimatum: Queer Love*. ("Can you believe—all this drama over a little bit of fingering?") When she finds out how sore my throat is after being intubated, she orders vegan soup from "Gwyneth Paltrow's favorite deli" and has her assistant drop off smoothies every morning.

Boys are always blowing up Samantha's phone. Girls, too, sometimes. I don't mind it, because when she's with me, she's *with* me, and she is with me more and more these days. One afternoon, I wake up in my nest of pillows to the sound of Sam sending a text in the other room. (Her most Boomer quality: using voice-to-text for absolutely everything.)

"I can't this week, period. Maybe next Thursday, question mark. Champagne emoji. No, not the words, the emoji. No, drinks emoji. No—"

Later, I tell her that she can go out if she wants to. "I'll be fine here!" I insist. "And I know I'm not the most riveting company at the moment."

"Have you met the people in this city? You're more interesting asleep than 95-percent of these dunces are on their best day." She kisses my forehead. "This is where I want to be."

By June, I'm almost fully healed, and Samantha invites me to accompany her to a beach party in the Hamptons. "It could be like a debutante ball for your new chest," she says, running her hand under my tank top. "A coming out party!"

I show up in my gayest trunks and an oversized t-shirt, while Samantha looks stunning in a miniscule scarlet bikini and a flowing, transparent caftan.

We greet her friends, and when, after several minutes, I still haven't taken off my shirt, Sam pulls me aside. "Ready?" she asks, squeezing my hands. I nod, even though I'm not sure

I am, and quickly pull my shirt over my head before walking back to the ladies. They are overly bright at my return.

"Wow, it's really like a man's chest!" Carrie exclaims.

"Carrie, you can't say that!" Miranda scolds.

"You can barely see the scars!" Charlotte coos.

Samantha looks straight at me. "Charlotte and Carrie are wrong; you can see the scars. And, honey, you are the hottest piece of ass on this whole goddamn beach. Do you think any of those boys over there"—she gestures vaguely at some oiled-up twinks sunbathing a few towels over—"would have the balls to do what you've done? Do you think any of these vapid shrews"—here, she gestures at her friends, ignoring their shocked glares—"have ever thought seriously about who they are and then fucking done something about it? I am in awe of you. And you are fucking gorgeous."

She grabs my hand and pulls me towards the water.

"C'mon, babe. Let's go swimming."

VÉRONIQUE EMMA HOUXBOIS

# Berenstain Brunch

ROSIE ACCOLA

# Reject Cognition, Embrace Carrie Bradshaw

I have never been able to meditate. The idea of letting my thoughts drift by on a lily pad without judgment has never worked for me. But I can watch *Sex and the City*, fully and presently, allowing my mind to empty out like Carrie dumping the contents of her oversized designer purse onto a table to find an elusive pack of cigarettes.

My friends and I call this "smooth brain time." The minute the theme song cues up, I am left with a narcotic sense of peace. I can physically feel the knots being untangled in my brain. I imagine this is how babies feel when they watch videos of cartoon blueberries bopping along to pop songs.

Watching *Sex and the City* feels like a wildly heterosexual pastime, like attending a bachelorette party in Nashville. It feels cheugy like monogrammed towels, but also luxurious and soft, like a fluffy robe from a nice hotel. I don't want to say that my problems fall away; rather, they are contained, like the color-coded designer gowns nestled in Carrie's closet.

Before I was a queer adult who viewed gender with an ambivalent shrug, I was a tween girl with a monthly subscription to *Teen Vogue*. While I was too young to watch *Sex and the City*, Carrie Bradshaw occupied the periphery of my cultural consciousness. The idea of making a living by writing a column for *Vogue* was everything I wanted and more.

By the time I started watching *SATC* in earnest, I was 27 years old and barely scraping by as a freelance writer. Before this, I'd considered *SATC* to be strictly hotel room viewing; I'd watch an occasional episode if it was on, but the show never stuck with me. Now, the quips Sarah Jessica Parker made as Carrie about the fickle nature of freelancing drew me into the show. I laughed out loud when Carrie glibly explained that she couldn't take time off for jury duty since she was her own boss. While the show's version of the financial instability of freelancing still looked like utter luxury compared to my scrounging for groceries, I still felt for Carrie, eating saltines in her apartment with her foot pressed against her knee as she paged through fashion magazines.

Three months into my ongoing *SATC* marathon, I experienced my first and only migraine. The pain was bad. It radiated down my entire spine; I thought I was having a stroke. As I waited for the Tylenol to kick in, contemplating whether I should go to urgent care, my mom suggested I watch an episode of *Sex and the City* to take the edge off. When the theme song queued up, I was struck by the horrifying realization that I genuinely loved this show. Here I was, having an absolute nightmare of a time, sleep-deprived and panicked but strangely comforted by Samantha and Carrie's inevitable back-and-forth about the allure of twenty-something guys.

A week later, I enrolled in an intensive outpatient therapy program to try and figure out my mental health and my meds once and for all. It was like school for emotions: eight hours a day trapped in a cinderblock room with other people who also wanted to die. The worst part was that I still wasn't sleeping. Not only was I emotionally exhausted, but I could barely keep my eyes open. When I returned home each night after treatment, however, I felt like I couldn't trust myself to relax. My favorite pastime, watching TV, filled me with dread. After struggling to stay awake all day, I suddenly became restless with the prospect of another sleepless night looming before me.

While I usually treasured my alone time, the prospect of hanging out solo seemed suddenly unbearable. I couldn't trust myself to sit still.

The other people in the program also admitted they were having a hard time being alone. "Try and do something nice for yourself," the therapist suggested. I spoke up for the first time all day: "Well, I guess I could order takeout and watch *Sex and the City*." The therapist's eyes lit up. "Exactly."

That night, I ordered sesame chicken from the Chinese place down the block and embarked on a hellbent mission to chill the fuck out for one second. I sat on the navy rug in my living room: my favorite spot, where I had spent the summer watching Carrie try and fail to procure a perfect first date. I nibbled on a red pepper soaked in Szechuan sauce as the Bossa Nova beats of the theme song spilled out from my TV.

*Could I really do this?* I felt the jittery, panicked anticipation of waiting for a plane to take off, and contemplated taking another anxious lap around my apartment. But I was also frustrated and starving. I gave myself a pep talk: *Jesus Christ, Rosie! Just watch your fucking show! You love it! Dammit, you love* Sex and the City*!*

In treatment, they talked a lot about the concept of radical acceptance, which is one of the core tenets of mindfulness. Radical acceptance posits that judging our present situation is the root of suffering. Instead, we should simply accept the current moment as-is. So, instead of panicking about the hell that would ensue when I tried to go to sleep, I focused on Carrie and the other girls. I let Stanford's quips lull me into a sense of docile complacency. When Samantha offered up a zinger about blow jobs ("I will wear whatever and blow whomever as long as I can breathe and kneel!"), I laughed out loud. My body relaxed for the first time in weeks.

One year after Carrie and the girls helped me through the worst week of my life, I started a full-time remote content writing job. Freelance writing wasn't cutting it anymore; the bulk of my income came from ghostwriting corny romance novels. I, a lesbian, was getting paid four cents per word to write smut about divorced dads with washboard abs. (Part of the reason why I started watching *SATC* in the first place was to acquaint myself with the language of hunks and messy-yet-lovable boyfriends.) Something had to change.

Now I spend business hours writing tech-adjacent content and nodding along during video meetings with my camera off. There are days where I miss freelancing; I still fantasize about the impossible luxury of my own $4/word column at *Vogue*. But I know that regardless of where I work or what I'm writing, my writing style will remain sly, slutty and a little dreamy, driven by a Sisphyean need to wonder. Maybe it's pointless, to shove a bedazzled boulder up a hill day after day, but it's what keeps me alive.

Besides, at the end of a particularly boring or long day, I can always return to *Sex and the City*. A few quick clicks, and I can once again feel Kim Cattrall press an ironing board over the wrinkles of my brain, leaving it pristine and refreshed, placid and smooth as the surface of an untouched Cosmopolitan.

# HAL DAVIS

I couldn't help but wonder: A Carrie Bradshaw found poem

infinite possibilities
went on and on ... I couldn't help wondering
about my own.
wondering
was
a form of
Hell but
I couldn't
exist without
the wonder
I couldn't help but wonder ...
I couldn't help but wonder if I really did know the way to let myself out.
I wondered ...
I wondered
I couldn't help but wonder what it meant that I wanted
I couldn't help but
fight myself
wide open

Taken from an online compilation of everything Carrie Bradshaw wondered about on *Sex and the City*, what started out as an exercise in exploring and satirizing Carrie's words ultimately became an earnest reflection on the trans experience of wondering yourself into existence.

M FLACK

# Shooting Hoops with My Buddy Steve

Scaling the steps out of the subway in a fog of sweat, I'm startled by the sight of bustling Big Apple streets above. Growing up in Tasmania, Australia's sleepy island state, has not prepared me for New York. The chaos of this city remains alien to me, despite the six months I've lived here. Something about New York will not make itself legible to me, and it seems intent on thrusting ahead whether I get it or not.

When I get to the bar, Layla greets me with a hug and gives a nod in the direction of the counter. "They're back!" Layla stage-whispers.

Rich divorced mums are always sidling up to the owner, Steve, trying to make a move on him, which Layla and I love to spectate. He has a shocking amount of allure for someone who seems to have had the same haircut since 1998. There's even a certain *je ne sais tboy* swag about the basketball shorts I see him wear sometimes. Perhaps he's . . . ? No—I really have a bad habit recently of projecting onto any hot 5-foot-something guy I can see.

"I think I can do better than those women."

Layla looks confused. "Sorry?"

"I think I can do better than those women, with Steve"

"I . . . How do you know this guy is gay?"

"There's nothing gayer than being a guy's guy. I'm just going to tell him I'm trying to start a social basketball group to meet people in the city."

Steve is radiating a beat-down, end-of-shift energy when I approach. He seems to look through me, rather than at me, as he asks for my order in his soft raspy voice. Before he can grab the glasses for Layla's and my beers, I muster my strength and force out the words:

"Hey, this is crazy, but I'm starting a social group just to shoot some hoops and meet people in the city—I was wondering if you would join us?" The words tumble out of my mouth and sit there on the bar between us.

"Huh. An old guy like me? It's been a while since I played—my old hoops buddy left the city years ago. I'd have to think about it."

"Let me put my number in your phone and you let me know what you think."

Heart pounding, I use his phone to text myself: *3 PM canal st courts, next tuesday*. I deliver his phone back to him via a sweaty palm and whip around to the door before he can say anything else.

A week later, I turn up to the court early, dressed in an outfit I thought too much about. (*Is this look too straight? Too Australian?*) I rush through what I remember of the drills I watched on TikTok, so focused that I don't notice Steve approaching. His thick, hairy thighs are revealed by disarmingly short shorts. This is already something I didn't plan for. The sun winks at me off his rimless glasses.

"Hey there, where's the gang?"

"Oh . . . everyone cancelled on me."

"That's too bad."

He chuckles. Steve seems more at ease than usual, away from the bar and whatever goes on at his house. He makes a goofy shot at the hoop a few meters away, missing by a generous amount.

Grinning sheepishly, he turns back to me. "Well, I guess it's just gonna be one-on-one?" he asks. "Yeow! Wouldn't like to be you."

I laugh, finally. "Don't talk too soon. I wouldn't want to show you up here and emasculate you or something."

"Buddy, get in line. Why do you think I stayed with my wife?"

I start dribbling the ball towards Steve, winding a path around him towards the top of the key at the other end of the court. I can't help but hold his gaze whenever our eyes meet, and this makes it even more difficult to remember how to keep the ball in my hand. When I miss on the first shot, he insists I take another.

It takes a few more, but when I finally swoosh the ball through the looming metal hoop, Steve converts our high-five slap into a hug, and I can't help but feel he's lingering. Either my horny, fresh-on-T imagination has gotten out of control, or this man is a lot more down to fuck than I expected.

Steve's command of the ball is more skilful than he initially let on. I can barely keep up with him, and all I can feel is my heart pounding and sweat drenching my shirt. When we pause for a second, I collapse into him. I swear I can feel him breathing in my sweaty musk before shrugging me upright again.

"Hey," he ventures, "how's about we take a break and cool off at the bar?"

The sumptuous bar is lit in late afternoon sun, and I stretch out in a booth while Steve pours us both a beer. Quickly getting impatient, I gesture for him to join me on my bench and take the drinks from him, putting them aside on the table before pulling him in for a long kiss. My hand forms a fist around his curls and he grunts softly at the tension.

He nods and pulls my face back towards his, his hands roaming downwards to trace the lines of my scars and then further into my shorts. His long fingers trace the outline of my clit through my drenched underwear and I want to scream. Steve's body, while a similar size, feels all-consuming against mine.

I tug off Steve's shirt and tell him to get up onto the table, where I remove his slutty little shorts and briefs to expose his swollen, pretty pink pussy peeking out from a mass of coarse black hair. I kneel down in front of him to bury my face in his smell, and when I lift my head up, I slap his exposed lips and clit. He yelps and looks up at me wide-eyed in delight.

Steve moves further back onto the table, knocking our beers over and spilling sticky golden liquid over both of us. We both laugh, and I lean forward to lick from his sharp collarbone to his ear.

After sucking some of the beer off my fingers, I tease the opening of his hole until, without warning, he grabs my hand and thrusts me deep inside. Seeing his back arc in pleasure as I move in and out of him, I add another finger, and another, his grunts deepening with each addition. Something about Steve's naked desire pulls pieces of me into alignment in an ecstatic way, manifesting someone I usually only glimpse momentarily. I straddle his thigh and grind my clit on him hard.

When I pull out of him, Steve looks up in confusion. His gaze turns to lust when he sees me spit in my open hand and tuck in my thumb. Holding his gaze, I ease in my fingers knuckle by knuckle. I'm not sure it's going to fit, until suddenly his hungry cunt has consumed my whole hand. Steve is hot and wet and convulsing around me, and as I work in and out of him, I use my free hand to stroke his clit. I can feel every little twitch in his pussy as he starts to come, gripping me so hard I start to feel pin pricks in my arm. As his gasps begin to slow, he pulls me down for a gentle kiss. Cradling my face in his hands, he whispers, "Ah, jeez."

Bobby Fine
starring in
I ♡ i love a charade
by Ollie Paige Linden
Bitsy von Muffling

Perplexing the Gays!
Go get 'em dear! ♡
I could grate cheese off those Abs!!!
Bewildering the Straights!
Don't call it love!
He's obvs Gay! what's she Thinking!?
Maybe they're in love?
who cares! what's the sex like!?

The show largely wants me to Feel bad for them...
...To believe they "settled" just b/c their relationship doesn't fit into the traditional mold.
*i haven't seen And Just Like That...
But watching them, I see nothing to pity.
They're having a great *time!
*so if anything in there invalidates this...no it doesn't!

DANIEL LANZA RIVERS

# "Best Is the Worst": A *SATC* History of My Hair

"I loved it, except for one huge problem: you have your leading lady running all over town wearing *a scrunchie!*" So begins Carrie's review of her lover Jack Berger's novel, *Hurricane Pandora.* After eight or so episodes of post-Aidan, single-Carrie ennui, our leading lady has fallen hard for a painfully self-conscious novelist who falls asleep listening to jungle sounds. Carrie has just finished her first read of Berger's 400-page commercial flop, and though she has plenty of glowing praise to share, this critique not only breaks Berger, but almost breaks their relationship.

Nowadays, I tend to find Carrie's stumble relatable—both as a writer who has been knocked back by a clear-eyed critique, and as a partner who has been guilty of picking at loose ends when I mean to be supportive. As a *SATC* fan, though, it's the scrunchie comment that's stayed with me over the years. Long before I started queering my pronouns and my wardrobe, I came to understand that scrunchies were pedestrian, gauche, and unworthy of a fashionable urban femme.

The first time I watched what I call "the scrunchie episode" (S6E4), I was a sophomore in college. After wearing my curly hair long in high school, I had begun cutting it short in a vague gesture toward boy drag that I hoped would make me more datable to the four other out queers at my suburban university. It was 2006, and I was a painfully self-conscious writer with a sincere streak. I owned all six seasons of *SATC* on DVD, and I fancied myself as something of a Carrie (didn't we all?).

By the time I moved to Jersey City to attend a Masters program I couldn't afford, short hair had become my new norm. A shy try-hard who wanted nothing more than to become a Great Novelist, I spent a year taking classes at a prestigious university that is notorious for saddling homosexuals with student loan debt. For nine months of that year, I interned at a literary agency in Midtown, where I lived out my New York literary fantasies by answering phones and combing the slush pile for a literary agent with a smart wardrobe, a severe bob, and a list of writers whom I idolized and adored. Like Carrie's editor at *Vogue*, this agent could be something of an inscrutable mentor, who said things like "You're so young!" and "Daniel reads everything!" in tones I would spend years fretting over.

As a shy, single queer living on the wrong side of the Hudson River in the early aughts, I felt adrift in New York's dating scene. A virgin who had moved from Sonoma County in a time before dating apps, I often felt like Carrie sitting at the bar at her own book party, reflecting on her abiding loneliness. My gender and my brain were still mysteries to me back then, and I experienced Manhattan with the lonely posture of a long-term tourist, someone who was more likely to sit at home watching *SATC* reruns than take the PATH train in for a date.

Though fun and bubbly, Carrie's deprecations could be exacting, especially for us queers who spent years internalizing them as mandates about how to be chic, datable, and sexy. I remember a moment in my PhD program when one of my classmates told me that he could never end an email with "Best." Apparently it was Big's regular signoff, which Carrie Bradshaw had once condemned by saying that "Best is the worst." I didn't much care about the critique back then, and it still strikes me as lacking in substance. But I can identify with feeling pinned in place by one of Carrie's pithy directives.

Thinking back on it now, I can't help but wonder if maybe Ann Coulter was onto something when she famously claimed that *Sex and the City* wasn't a show about women, but was instead about homosexual men. Coulter is wrong and hateful in plenty of ways, but her misreading inadvertently illuminates the way that *SATC* served as a kind of diagonal queer representation in the homophobic television landscape of the late nineties and early aughts. Whatever straight, cis, white-woman bullshit she dragged along with her, Carrie Bradshaw was one of us—or at least, she was as close to one of us as we were allowed to see onscreen. And I'd hazard a guess that many of us have our own admonitions from the show that have followed us through the years, shaping our sense of fashion, possibility, and self-expression.

It doesn't bother me to say that coming into my gender later in life has meant learning to embrace elements of my own girlhood that I've overlooked or left fallow. As someone who has spent my life habitually downplaying my own care (I know, I'm working on it), I've had to teach myself the arts of girlhood with help from sweet friends, a supportive partner, and books on hair-braiding with girls who look like my nieces on the cover. After some initial hesitation (thanks, Carrie), scrunchies have become a standard part of my wardrobe. I've assembled a broad collection, and probably wear them five days a week, often using them to toss together a casual asymmetrical hair style that keeps my curls from latching onto my beard.

I'm 40 now, and I've learned that I'm more of a 6-foot-3-inch blend of Carrie and Miranda: a business femme with a backlog of publications and a book contract, who is prone to stress-eating at the kitchen counter. My curly auburn hair is longer than it has ever been, and it plays off of the white streak that bisects my ginger beard. My shoulders are the width of a small truck, and I can't afford designer outfits, so I mostly shop online where I can find sizes to accommodate my build and my curving lines. Thanks to years of practice, and the settling of middle age, I've learned not to give a fuck if some straight, cis woman wants to tell me that my fashion looks too earnest or pedestrian.

Looking back at my New York year sometimes feels like peering through a fog. My younger self, my own aspiring Carrie, tends to come through in blurs of memories and sensations: climbing the steps to my internship in some colorful boyish outfit, visiting Walter de Maria's *Earth Room* and breathing in the aura of living soil, listening to my Walkman on the PATH train home after drinks with my classmates, and attending my first NYC literary reading.

I arrived at that reading over an hour early, and posted up at the bar with a history of the Triangle Shirtwaist Factory fire (homework for my first semester of grad school). Public events have always brought out the introvert in me, and the book was something of a social deflection, an invisibility spell that cloaked me as the event time drew near and the venue filled with trendy patrons. A woman with a severe bob took the seat next to me, ordered a drink, and broke the spell by asking about my book. She was warm, confident, and friendly. I didn't yet know that she represented my Favorite Writer, the one I'd come out to see. Or that she would interview me for an internship just a few weeks later, and be the one who taught me the easy efficiency of ending my work emails with "Best." I still don't know how she feels about scrunchies—though, in truth, I've never seen her wear one. It's probably a reach to say that she influenced my sense of style, but she did transform my sense of possibility and my understanding of the writing life. A single woman with a successful literary agency named after her, she would eventually dislodge Carrie's authority over the life I dreamed of. But all of that would come later, through months of conversation and collaboration and the stumbling embarrassments of working my first office job. That night we were just a couple of New York singles, sharing a drink and talking books at a trendy bar while we waited for a writer we loved to take the stage.

SERENA HOMMES

# Sex and the City:

## The Roleplaying Game

In this game, you roleplay as cosmopolitan socialites in a long-running television series about people living a utopian existence in The Big City (any city). You have your dream job, you never worry about rent, and your work-life balance is perfect. You have a limitless credit card just for shoes and eating out. The only area in which you struggle is sex and relationships. Sexual, platonic, romantic, or any kind of relationship: that is the area in which your needs are not quite being met. At least you have your best friends for company.

To play this game you will need:

- Friends, acquaintances, or strangers with whom to play (four is a good number)
- Something to write with/on
- Food and drinks (optional)
- A six-sided die (optional)

### Talking Phase 1

You and your fellow socialites meet up for a kiki. Do you get brunch, or just drinks? Takeout, or New York's hottest restaurant? Set the scene together, and *always* tell us what you are wearing. Introduce yourself as your character. Ask each other questions and compare your experiences.

Here are some questions you can ask yourself to get into your character:

- What do you do for work?
- For pleasure?
- Have you ever been in love?
- Martini straight up, or with a twist? (u fruity?)

Most importantly, we want to know what is going on in your character's sex and dating life. Could it be:

- Not enough sex?
- Too much sex?
- There is no one?
- There are too many to choose?
- They're perfect but they don't share your kink?
- How can anyone that gorgeous be straight?

### Journal Phase

In this phase, your characters each go out for the night. Take a few minutes to individually write about what your character does out on the town. You could set a time limit of 10 minutes or so, or just write until you fill a page. Anything could happen! Do you find the courage to tell your crush/

date/friend/ex how you really feel? Or learn that what you desired isn't really what you want after all? Ask yourself:

- Where did you go?
- With whom?
- What did they say?
- How did you do it?
- *What did you wear?*

If you need inspiration, roll a six-sided die and use the table below to determine what unexpectedly occurs:

1. A bus featuring your photo splashes you with road water
2. You run into your crush's ex
3. An artist asks you to pose for a tasteful depiction of your genitalia
4. You run into an old flame
5. You're invited to a gender reveal
6. You trip and fall but a charming stranger catches you

### Talking Phase 2

When everyone's done writing, it's time to gather for another brunch/meal/round of drinks, either at the same place as Phase 1 or somewhere else. Take turns telling your fellow players what happened. It's okay to read straight from what you wrote, or to just tell it how you remember it. Ask each other follow-up questions or for more dirty details. Would you have handled the situation differently? Maybe your story evolves as you hear from your friends. Were you actually at the same club? Did you see the same person? It's okay if your recollection changes, but don't lie to your besties.

### The End

Your episode does not need to have a resolution. You can keep playing for an entire season, create a spin-off, or let this one just be a pilot episode. It's up to you! After all, you are the star.

**Midtown * Aidan's Cabin * Steve's bar * Hoboken**

**fuck buddy:**

Che Diaz

Sean (the bisexual)

Samantha Jones

Smith Jerrod

**future ex:**

Steve Brady

Maria (the lesbian painter)

Skipper

Trey MacDougal

**best friend:**

Seema Patel

Stanford Blatch

Anthony Marentino

Lisa Todd Wexley

**# of shoes you own:**

5,000

2

A reasonable 100

Whatever fits in your oven

**secret weakness:**

Post-its

The Rabbit

Magda

You can't help but wonder

**job:**

Journalist

Art curator

Lawyer

Public relations

**worst moment:**

Falling on the runway

Farting in bed

Dyeing your pubes

Being left at the altar

**best moment:**

Your they mitzvah

Mr. Big dying

Liza officiating your wedding

Honeymooning with friends

**queer/transphobic catchphrase:**

"Can you wake up a lesbian?"

"Trendy by day. Tranny by night"

"Pick a side and stay there!"

"Your friendly neighborhood pre-op transexual hooker"

**If you're a Charlotte, use the biggest digit of your phone #**
**If you're a Samantha, use the first digit of the # of people you've slept with**
**If you're a Miranda, use the number of hours you work a day**
**If you're a Carrie, use your shoe size**

JUNO CARMEL

# Party Rock Anthem

Being nonbinary is pretty embarrassing. I don't mean that in a self-hating or shameful way; it's just a circumstance that simultaneously garners a lot of attention and gets a bad rap—like driving a Prius, being vegan, or earnestly posting on LinkedIn. To be nonbinary is to take on the onus of constantly bringing up your own pronouns and accepting awkward apologies from people who can't understand how to use them. It's a life sentence of hearing cringeworthy terms like "enby" and "auncle" and "joyfriend."

It also means that you naturally take note of every real or fictional they/them who exists in the public eye. You begin noticing what Sam Smith is wearing at award shows, or praying that Cole Escola's popular Broadway show is actually funny (thankfully, it is). It's only natural to Google things like "Demi Lovato detransition" or "Halsey pronouns," and keep mental tabs on various celebrities who are showing early signs of nonbinary behavior. And truly, if I don't remember the comically irrelevant nonbinary character in Disney's *Elemental*, who will? (Their name is Lake Ripple, if you even care.)

So naturally, we must discuss the hyper-woke reboot of *Sex and the City*. When *And Just Like That . . .* debuted on HBO in 2021, they replaced Samantha Jones with an assortment of new sidekicks, including some of the worst nonbinary representation the world has ever seen.

For those of us who exist in homosexual circles, Che Diaz is a familiar nightmare—a queer archetype reminiscent of your worst ex, who constantly posts embarrassing thirst traps and proudly wears attire from the Target Pride collection. Though it's bad enough that Che is a polyamorous podcaster and stand-up comedian, their personality is somehow even more painful. They give Miranda the odd nickname "Rambo," and make jokes like, "Last year I dated this woman who was transitioning . . . transitioning from nice person to asshole!" They're also horny in the weirdest contexts; they famously finger Miranda in Carrie's kitchen while Carrie is bedridden post-surgery.

On one level, Che is hateable because they're a terrible face for the they/them community—why would anyone want to be represented in the media by someone whose main traits are being horny and corny? But the more disappointing thing about Che is that the character feels hollow, like the writers got all of their ideas about nonbinary people from one neurotic corner of TikTok. Sure, I can list a bunch of cringey things that Che has done, but I truly don't know anything about them beyond their obsessions with fame and identity politics. What are their dreams beyond casting Tony Danza as their dad in *Che Pasa*? Why is Che even interested in dating Miranda, a late-in-life lesbian who's battling alcoholism while going through a midlife career change and a long-overdue divorce? How can someone simultaneously suck all of the air out of the room *and* be boring?

Unsurprisingly, Che proved so unpopular that the writers cut the character out of the show by the end of season 2. But even in profound darkness, there must be a glimmer of light. Though the *SATC* universe is a terrible place to find decent LGBTQ representation, the reboot humbly offers us another they/them to consider: Charlotte's nonbinary child, Rock.

Initially introduced (aka born) in *Sex and the City: The Movie*, Rock has since grown into a chill tween. In *ALJT*'s first season, Rock alarms their Upper East Side parents by adopting a new, profoundly nonbinary name. When Charlotte finds out about Rock's new name and pronouns from a squad of PTA moms, she asks Rock why they wouldn't tell the family first.

"I did let you know; I put up a TikTok," Rock casually explains, not looking up from their video game.

"Yo! My name is Rock, the new kid on the block," they chant in the video, wearing quintessential nonbinary attire (a backwards baseball cap and a striped rugby shirt). "Not tryna shock, or joinin' the flock. R-O-C-K, Rock!"

Harry and Charlotte both struggle with the change for a few episodes, questioning whether their kid is serious or just looking for attention. ("Is Rock your rapper name?" a bewildered Harry asks after seeing the TikTok.) Rock's immediate character arc is a bit two-dimensional—they want to cut their hair short and wear boyish clothes and redecorate their side of the room—but their actions send a clear-enough message to their family.

By the end of season 1, Charlotte has rebranded Rock's bat mitzvah as a "they mitzvah," which really should be called a b'nai mitzvah, but whatever. Rock is severely unprepared for the event (#nonbinaryexcellence), which leads Trans

Rabbi Hari Nef™ to suggest that they either cut Rock's Torah portion down to two lines or do the whole thing in English.

"I did not convert to Judaism to have my child be 'they mitzvahed' in English," Charlotte snaps, with wrinkles in her botoxed forehead.

Rock's they mitzvah is everything a queer could dream of: beefy gays drop off 130 loaves of challah while wearing rainbow pride yarmulkes; Trans Rabbi Hari Nef™ has to rush to a Bushwick wedding after the ceremony; Rock wears an oversized pink suit and ultimately refuses to get mitzvah'd.

"I don't want to be labeled as anything," Rock tells their parents. "Not as a girl, or boy, nonbinary, a Jew, Christian, Muslim, or even a New Yorker." When Charlotte asks them if they're just "nothing," they give a cheesy-but-valid answer: "I'm only 13. Can't I just be me?"

Throughout the second season, Rock mostly hangs out around the house in funky oversized shirts and bucket hats and a gold serpentine chain. They get scouted for a Ralph Lauren ad while skateboarding in the park, but later turn down offers from major modeling agencies because they don't feel like doing that anymore. They also start saying woke teenager things like, "I won't be party to upholding the patriarchy and the heteronormative standards of beauty," which assures me that they will fit in just fine at LaGuardia High School and whatever small liberal arts college they get into.

Even with significantly less screen time than Che, Rock's interior world simultaneously feels more expansive and understandable than their older counterpart. They're defiant and silly and act like a real teenager who's learning and growing and sometimes trying on personas that don't quite fit them. In not doing too much, the writers accidentally created a realistic nonbinary character who doesn't embarrass the whole community every time they open their mouth.

And personally? I think that rocks.

MIRANDA J

## R-O-C-K Rock & Rocks

# EM SOLAROVA

# Love Note:

## How making the coffee and getting the lunches made me fall in love with the silly world of *SATC/AJLT*

As I write this essay in October 2024, I currently work as an office production assistant on season 3 of *And Just Like That . . .* Make no mistake, my decision-making powers start and end with "what flavor of seltzer will be stocked in the office fridge today"—and even there, everyone can veto me. I make coffee and order lunches and change the toner and go to the DMV so other people don't have to.

When I got the job, it was just that: a job. Having grown up in Europe without HBO and with a sweeping disdain for anything girly or feminine, I was unmarked by *Sex and the City*'s cultural significance. I remained untouched by it until early covid lockdowns, when a mix of boredom, professional interest, and curiosity about this cultural behemoth led me to start watching. (By then, I had realized I was trans, which meant I could stop making it my entire personality to differentiate myself against anything feminine and was free to explore the *SATC* universe.)

I only made it through a handful of episodes, however, before stopping in disgust. I couldn't understand what made

*SATC* so great. How was this show pushing the envelope? It was so painfully white and straight and, for a show about sex, extraordinarily vanilla! The way they talked about bisexuality as if it wasn't real! The way they couldn't handle foreskin or even the mention of anal! Though I enjoyed watching the parade of boyfriends played by now-famous actors, from Gabriel Macht and Bradley Cooper to Will Arnett and Justin Theroux, I didn't feel the need to keep watching.

I didn't give *Sex and the City* another try until after I started working on *And Just Like That . . .* One of my favorite things about working in film and television is being able to connect the dots and see how everything comes together. Knowing the characters and their storylines (and their apartments and closets) makes my days much more interesting when I am, say, dealing with the delivery of Richard Burton's dog bed.

To my surprise, I found myself really enjoying the show! I was invested in the characters and could appreciate the humor and the ridiculous situations with a different perspective. I think adjusting my expectations and looking at the show as what it is, and not an over-inflated idea I had made up in my head, played a big part in this. I had also recently become a New Yorker, which further bolstered my understanding and appreciation.

That being said, the real magic of working on *AJLT*—which I now hold in a special soft place in my heart—are the people I have met. The cast and crew are not only skilled and dedicated, but also kind, generous, and a genuine pleasure to be around for 12+ hours a day.

Now, when I watch *AJLT*, I see reminders of our hard work all over the screen. I remember personal life details, such as the scene we shot on the day I got an eye infection, or the day when Sweetgreen ran out of avocado. (A real emergency: I had to get avocados from the grocery store and slice them for everyone's salads.) I notice the floor tile and think of the wonderful people who made sure that, despite delivery delays, it was ready for its moment of fame under the shoes of Carrie Bradshaw. I see the supporting actor with whom I once chatted in the elevator, and I remember the costumer who made sure their colorful scarf sat perfectly across their shoulders for every take. When I see a certain character's sunglasses, I know that those shades were accidentally delivered to the wrong address, and I had to hunt them down based on nothing but a proof-of-delivery photo that showed the tile and baseboard of some apartment building lobby in Astoria.

One of my most cherished memories is the time I delivered a giant cake to celebrate an actor's milestone on set. I saw his face light up in real time as he recognized the thoughtful, personalized decoration, and then excitedly explained the backstory to the whole crew.

There was also the time an actor's lunch was late. Just as they were being ushered out to their car service, I was able to catch the delivery, find their order, and bring it to them. For the rest of the season, this person would always greet me with a big smile, exchanging a knowing glance about the importance of chana saag.

Similarly, I was once asked to deliver script pages to set across the lot. I arrived to find their recipient pouncing for them with an excited "just in time!" At the wrap party, this highly-regarded crew member pulled me aside and told me that I truly came through for them because had I not arrived right then, the whole day would have been delayed.

Being thanked for excelling at your entry-level job by the accomplished, the famous, and the fabulous may not sound like much, but from my experience, it's quite rare. Maybe I'm a sucker for letting it charm me, but on many other shows I've worked on, we were yelled at for doing our jobs poorly and ignored when we did them well. So, yes, I'll admit that being acknowledged for my hard work makes me appreciate my job more. When the people in charge recognize the importance of the coffee runs, lunches, and seltzers, it shows me how integral I am to the whole operation.

This attitude has unlocked my ability to see the magic contained within my daily tasks. A prime example of this is making "the sides." These are vital documents to the daily set operations; they include information for every department as to what elements are needed, as well as the scripts for that day's work. Every night I would print, cut, collate, and staple these before organizing them into envelopes for the next day. They are watermarked with everyone's names, and looking at these names regularly made me reflect on all of the talented, hard-working, and truly incredible people whom I met on this job. I enjoyed being able to see my work through this lens. I'm sorry to be a simp to my menial, entry-level job, but, at the risk of sounding like capitalism's happiest little footsoldier, I like to focus on the good things in my life, and I am grateful that the *AJLT* office has provided many opportunities for finding joy.

While I might not call *And Just Like That . . .* my favorite show, I don't have to like every single plot point or quippy line in order to appreciate how I've learned and grown while working on the show. I also admire how much the show means to its audience; millions of exhausted people around the world can temporarily forget their troubles as they watch Carrie, Miranda, Charlotte, LTW, and Seema. After all, the show's biggest appeal is wish fulfillment—not just in terms of material luxury, but in terms of female friendship. Sure, viewers love the shoes, the clothes, the apartments, the restaurants, and the sex, but that can all easily be seen elsewhere and changes every season. *Sex and the City*'s decades-lasting magic is these women's enduring support for each other through life's many twists and turns.

. . . And I like to remember that when I'm stuck in traffic bringing someone an iced latte from another borough.

AOIFE SMITH

# Brooklyn Butch Thirst Trap

In your hand-me-down
floor-length mirror, in your

forest green boxer briefs. Your arm
bending and stretching up towards

your face with slow movement.
Following the arch of your left bicep,

I flow to the turn of your wrist. To
your hand. Your fingers entangled

in your hair. Freshly home
from your closing shift, you're

getting ready to shower. I ask what
you're up to when the day has been

washed from skin, if you want
anything from the bodega on 86th.

GEORGIA MILLS

# Girl, Haunted

In the *Sex and the City* episode "My Motherboard, Myself" (S4E8), Carrie's computer breaks and Miranda's mother dies.

Each of the women respond to Miranda's mother's death differently: Carrie lashes out, Charlotte sends flowers, and Samantha shuts down. When Carrie tearfully breaks the news over breakfast, we see Samantha go someplace else. She dissociates; her eyes unfocus. During sex, she loses her orgasm ("in the cab?" Carrie chides later), and in Samantha's distress we see something deeper: her fear of death, under her sex-fuelled zest for life.

Rewatching *Sex and the City*, I've been thinking about the work that it takes to become the person you want to be. Throughout the show, Samantha occasionally shares details about her life before moving to New York: serving dilly bars at Dairy Queen when she was fifteen; getting an abortion alone in college; how her mother was saddled with "three kids and a drunk husband" by the time she was Samantha's age.

Samantha's past is buried underneath her glamorous and professional exterior, whereas Carrie lives as though she's still the younger version of herself: the Connecticut teen who dreamed of moving to the city. She parties until dawn and loses track of time, romanticizing New York and Mr. Big, coffee and cigarettes. Time and time again, Carrie is rescued from her mess—breakups and financial issues and fights with friends—via magical thinking and impossible HBO luck. "In real life, the city would eat her up," my friend said as we sat outside a coffee shop in sweats on a Sunday, dreading the workweek.

I feel embarrassed when I act like Carrie, giving my inner teenager access to my bank account and body, letting her drive the car towards shiny lights and buzzy thrills. Waking up hungover at 23 from tequila, and the recollection of what she drove me to, the mortification that comes the morning after crying in the back of an Uber for reasons only she knows, I don't (ughgod), holding onto the side door and seeing stars, stumbling up the stairs home in a tangle of jangling keys and earbuds and heel straps and text messages, laying on my back on the cold linoleum floor, eyes closed, breathing. I never really find the feeling that I'm looking for on a restless night out. I'm seeking to soothe pent-up frustrations; to exorcise the banal demons ("nobody talks about backing up; my computer died"); to distract from the fact that being a writer with a column is an unreal dream, that it takes two jobs and weekly therapy and expensive chemical face wash to "keep it together."

The stable life that Samantha has built for herself allows her to live comfortably, and she works hard to take care of herself. She knows how to play the game to get what she wants. She owns an eponymous PR agency and a loft in the Meatpacking district. ("See, New York? We have it all," she toasts over a bottle of champagne upon moving in.) When Carrie needs $30,000 to buy her apartment because her building goes co-op, Samantha offers to loan her half the money.

Over martinis and chocolate cake with the girls, Samantha declares that she's never cried at work. Carrie says that she cried to her editor when she missed a deadline—she claimed to be having problems at home, but in reality, she was sunning in the Hamptons.

"That makes the rest of us look bad," Miranda scoffs.

"Oh boohoo, it was 80 degrees and sunny," Carrie says, shoveling cake into her mouth.

Carrie obsessively labors over her relationships, feelings, and memories. She splays out on her bed, writing about her experiences, reliving moments alone in her room. Her life is still my fantasy. It's easier, in that it takes less effort, to let yourself be driven by your emotions, without doing the work to resist your impulses. (Sending a stream of texts in an anxious moment; staying out too late.) But indulging in this way of being doesn't feel cute or fun anymore—letting myself live like Carrie, in the real world, creates a vicious cycle of regret. Chaos and drama, forgetting bill payments and birthdays.

Through Carrie's neurotic personality, I see a baby woman searching for a magical concept of love in a princess dreamworld. This is why, when her sense of reality is shattered—by a broken computer, a broken heart—she wants time to stand still for her sadness.

Five more minutes, something I've always said. I just want five more minutes.

Carrie's constant rumination contrasts Samantha's fear of slowing down. Samantha lies about her age; she gets plastic surgery. She loves work and sex and parties and being present in the moment. She seems to have a pervasive awareness of time passing, and a deep fear of looking in the rearview mirror, of pulling over. When Charlotte says that she wants to quit her job to have a baby and volunteer at her husband's hospital, Samantha tells her to be "damn sure before you get off the Ferris wheel, because the women waiting to get on are 22, perky, and ruthless." Imparting this wisdom is Samantha's way of mothering her friends. Underneath her advice is her fear of powerlessness, of getting stuck in a mediocre life. "You have to grab 35 by the balls," she says on Carrie's 35th birthday.

Miranda's mother's death comes suddenly and unexpectedly, with lots of realistic practicalities attached. The day of the funeral, while Miranda is shopping for a "shitty black dress," a matronly saleswoman informs her, unsolicited, that she's been buying the wrong bra size.

"I think I know! What's best, for me!" Miranda snaps at the woman now tugging expertly on her bra straps. Then, after a pause, she blurts out an explanation: "I'm sorry. My mother just died, and—"

The saleswoman's face folds knowingly as she wordlessly embraces Miranda, who melts into her shoulder. Through the screen: the stillness of a moment that feels good and heavy and long, like a warm nap. Close your eyes, stay forever (five more minutes).

At the funeral, while Charlotte and Carrie say all of the right things, Samantha can't summon the words to acknowledge the death at all, awkwardly complimenting Miranda and looking around uncomfortably in her seat. During the service, she breaks, locking eyes with Miranda across the pews, mouthing "I'm sorry" as she begins to inconsolably sob.

Samantha's emotional turmoil in "My Motherboard, Myself" reminds me of a previous episode, "All or Nothing" (S3E10). Sam gets the flu and insists that Carrie come over to make her mother's "cure-all" childhood concoction: Fanta and cough syrup blended over ice. In her feverish state, Samantha cries over not having a boyfriend to fix her curtain rod. ("We're all alone, Carrie.") She's crying for longings that she didn't know she felt: for what her mother wasn't able to give her—a stable home and a solid foundation—and the particular sadness that comes from craving a deep comfort that you've never had, as an adult in your own apartment.

Later, when she's feeling better, Samantha brushes her crying jag off with a joke about how sick she was, her voice as taut as an old movie star's. I wonder if that's what it takes for her to be the woman she wants to be every day—her sense of reservation, a lack of emotion. To not be like her mother.

After her emotional exorcism in church, Samantha comes during sex.

"[You have to] confront the ghost, acknowledge its presence, then release it," she says earlier in the season, when Miranda thinks that her apartment is haunted. "Everybody knows that."

# Acknowledgements

**Tuck & Niko:**

First and foremost, thank you so much to our 45 incredible contributors. This book would not exist without your genius and creativity, and it's an honor to collaborate with you. Thank you also to the many talented people whose pitches and submissions we couldn't fit into this book.

Many thanks as always to Casey Plett and the LittlePuss Press crew for teaching us how to do any of this. Thank you also to Oliver & Ashley at Metonymy Press for adopting us in Canada, and to everyone else who has helped us get our little books out into the world.

Thank you to Jakob Vala for transforming 50 Google Docs into one beautiful, book-shaped book. An icon, a legend. And thanks to Mattie Lubchansky for giving Carrie irreversible damage!

To the queer freaks of the world: thank you, love u, this is for you.

**Tuck:**

After we published *2 Trans 2 Furious*, we spent a year searching for the perfect Richly Gendered Text for our second anthology. Thank you to Sarah Esocoff for suggesting *Sex and the City* when we hung out in HVK that one time. You were so correct.

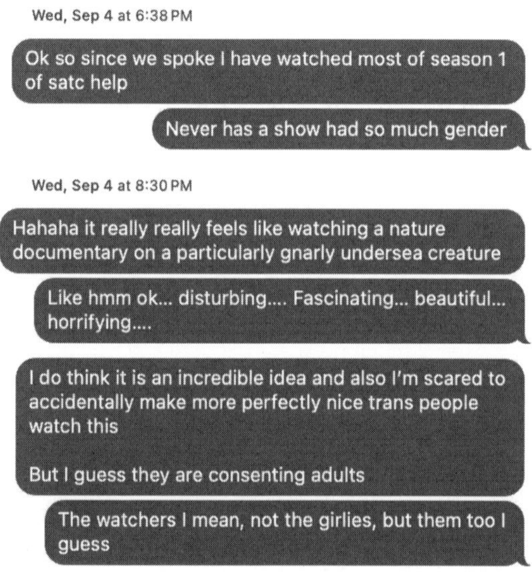


Thank you to Niko for working so hard on this book even though she had her own debut memoir to worry about!!! (Her book is *The Dad Rock That Made Me a Woman* and it rules and I hope you read it immediately.)

Thank you to Calvin, Chae, Conner, and MJ for your editing and publishing wisdom, and for listening to me talk about *Sex (Change) and the City* for a year. Thanks also to J for his patience as I fill our Brooklyn apartment with hundreds of copies of Girl Dad Press books. And hey, thank *you* for buying this book and thus improving the apartment clutter situation! You're a hero.

To Sabs, Kendra, Maddy, Emma, Kelsey, Torrey, and Bobby: Thank you for saying such kind words about *SCATC* on a ridiculously condensed timeline. You are all angels!

Finally, thank you to Cynthia Nixon. No particular reason; I just feel like she deserves it.

**Niko:**

I would like to thank Tuck Woodstock for taking on the brunt of the labour on this collection, for putting up with me while I lost my mind releasing an entirely different book, and for the vision and clarity of thought to stand by the idea that queer and trans people deserve to make beautiful art about whatever silly bullshit they desire. Thanks to all the writers, artists, poets, game makers, and more for all your hard work on this, and thanks to everyone who reads it.

Thank you, New York City, you're the fifth character of my heart.

# Contributors

**A.M. Goodhart** is a Madison, WI-based writer and textile artist. They have published poems in *Epiphany*, *The Indianapolis Review*, *Grist*, and *Lake Effect*. Their collection *Neither Kind of Body* was a semi-finalist for the A. Poulin, Jr. Poetry Prize and the Pamet River Prize.

**Addye Susnick** is a researcher, educator, facilitator, and copy editor based in Vancouver, Canada. They are currently a PhD candidate at the University of British Columbia, where their dissertation explores trans joy as a political feeling, as well as a collective member and avid volunteer at Spartacus Books.

If Kristin Davis is reading this, **Adrian Matias Bell** is a huge fan, and sorry if this weirded you out. If Michael Patrick King is reading this, he's not sorry at all. And if David Eigenberg is reading this, Adrian's free on Thursday—call him. www.ajmb.info

**Alex Bedder** is a writer, artist, and performer. They live in Brooklyn, NY.

**Amy Zimmerman** is a writer and bookseller based in upstate New York.

**aoife smith** is a poet and fiber artist based in Brooklyn. Currently, he is pursuing an MFA and making a lot of zines. His work has appeared in print and online. Butches, daddies, and especially butch-daddies, can find aoife on Instagram @aoife_is_laughing.

**Ariana Martinez** is a freelance film critic and culture writer earning their MA in Film Studies at UIowa. Their interests include the 1980s, romance, and death—on and off screen. You can follow their work at awakeintheam.com.

**Bri LeRose** is an LA and Milwaukee-based comedy writer and director. Bri is the co-writer of the award-winning film *The People's Joker*. She has written for several TV series and directed Maria Bamford's acclaimed stand-up special *Local Act*.

**Chae Sung (성채연)** is a wintertime writer, a summertime ice cream maker, and a weekend bisexual. They are working on a collection of poems about accumulation, density, and grief, and an essay collection about sex, masculinity, love, and violence. They live in New York (not Brooklyn), where they dream up little projects and hang out with their friends.

**Conner Reed** is a gay guy who lives in Brooklyn. Right now, he edits book reviews at *Publishers Weekly*.

**Cooper Bedin** (they/them) is a weird little freak. They dream of living with 15 cats. They are passionate about problematic reality television.

**Dani Janae** is a dyke poet from Pittsburgh, PA. Her work has appeared in *INTO*, *Xtra*, *Vice*, *Refinery29*, and elsewhere. Her debut collection of poetry, *Hound Triptych*, will be published by Sundress Publications in Spring 2026. She lives in South Carolina.

**Daniel Lanza Rivers** is a queer, nonbinary writer and professor who lives in the San Francisco Bay Area with their partner Rowan and three cats. A 2024 Lambda Literary Fellow in Creative Nonfiction, Daniel's writing has appeared in Terrain.org, the *SF Chronicle*, *American Quarterly*, and others. Daniel's first book, *California Futures*, is forthcoming from Duke University Press.

**Diana Schlossberg** is diarist, performer, director, Charlotte, and designer from Chicago. Her solo performance works, *On Diary* (2022) and *Be Me or My Mom* (2024), have been presented at Bowery Poetry Club (CH-V) and The Tank. She lives in Bushwick. dianab.diary@gmail.com

**Drew Thelke** is an artist and educator living in Madison, WI. They hold two ceramics degrees, write short stories, and draw silly pictures.

**Em Solarova** is a nonbinary filmmaker, writer, and cat lad(y) based in New York City. They are currently working on a comedy series about queer (sex) life with focus on its undeniable joy, inherent humor, and infallible awkwardness.

**Fancy Feast** is a Brooklyn-based burlesque performer, sex educator, and author of *Naked: On Sex, Work, and Other Burlesques.* Her work has been featured in *Vogue*, *HuffPost*, and the *Washington Post*, and she performs at venues including the Metropolitan Opera, the Whitney, and in dirty little backrooms all over the country.

**Flórián Dracula** (they/them) is a citizen librarian, transsexual ~artist~, horror writer, and migraine-haver living the dream in Southern California. Their work has previously appeared in *Write-or-Die Magazine* and *Coffin Bell.*

**Georgia Mills** is a writer based in Toronto, ON. More importantly, she's a Carrie sun, Charlotte moon, and Enid rising (IYKYK).

**Hal Davis** is a cat dad and TV enthusiast from Little Rock, AR. They are the co-founder of Wig Dog Press, a southern queer print-making trio whose work can be found on Instagram @wigdogpress.

**Harron Walker** is a writer who lives in Brooklyn. She is the author of *Aggregated Discontent: Confessions of the Last Normal Woman*, a new essay collection from Random House, and Veronica Place, a forth-coming novella-slash-primetime soap pastiche from TigerBee Press.

**Jas Brown** is a queer and trans cat whisperer who lives on Lekwungen lands in Victoria, BC. They are an avid scholar of television, watcher of the stars, and consumer of noodles. They also credit tongue-thruster Miranda Hobbes for their decision to get braces in high school.

**Jesse Robkin** is the head writer for the YouTube channel Tolarian Community College and a regular writer elsewhere. Her debut short film *Stress Fracture* is streaming on Open Television. She lives in Brooklyn.

**Julian Palacios** (he/him) has been described as "the tboy of Meanjin (i.e. so-called Brisbane, Australia)" at least once. He lives, writes, and cavorts with his boyfriend, gay cat, and dyke dog. You can find his photography & future creative endeavours on Instagram @antisocialmorays.

**Juno Carmel** is a born-and-raised New Yorker who used to identify as a Samantha/Carrie but is now transgender. Their writing has appeared in the *New York Times*, *Los Angeles Times*, and *Washington Post*. They currently live in Los Angeles with their partner, Re, and a pet lizard named Cher.

**K3** is your local transexual DTF dyke-to-fag bisexual. An admirer of hard-working women, with a profound love for lesbians.

**Kit Mills** is a comic artist and illustrator living in Brooklyn with a really small cat.

**M Flack** is an archivist by day, archivist by night. They live in Melbourne, Australia, with their two housemates and one FIV+, toothless cat.

**Malachi Boling** is a writer who cooks a lot. His submission of yet more Steve-based erotica was rejected and this is the result.

**mattie lubchansky** is a cartoonist and illustrator living in beautiful Queens, NY. She is the author of *Boys Weekend* and *Simplicity*.

**mb bischoff** is a poet and programmer in Brooklyn, NY. She's soft, trans, and online at mbbischoff.com. Her favorite color is red.

**Miranda J** is just here, man, loving rocks.

**Montreal "Monty" Benesch** is a linguist and artist currently based on Chumash land. Their work includes co-curating *trans*languaging*, an art show by multilingual trans artists about their relationships with their languages. You can find that at transxlanguaging.wordpress.com and find them at montrealbenes.ch.

**mx feelings** has spent equal hours of his life watching *Sex and the City* as swimming, sleeping, and being in love. This submission was written in one go on a break at work—a gruesome tale of what can happen to the trans faggot if left without direction.

**Niko Stratis** is an award-winning/losing writer, the author of *The Dad Rock That Made Me a Woman*, the co-host of *The OC, Again* podcast, and the co-editor of *2 Trans 2 Furious*, which won a Lambda Award she never actually got in the mail. She lives in Toronto, which is basically the New York of Canada.

**Nina Katz** is a writer based in Albuquerque, NM. In 2006, their mom wore the same dress Miranda wears on the *Sex and the City* movie poster to their brother's bar mitzvah party, and they have never stopped talking about it. @ninatummyache

**Ollie Paige Linden** is a nonbinary artist and avid TV watcher currently based in Tucson, AZ.

**Ozzy Llinas Goodman** is an audio producer and writer based in Brooklyn. By day, they're *Gender Reveal*'s senior producer and resident horror expert. By night, they trawl the content mines looking for fictional characters to inject with HRT. You can follow them on Instagram @ozzy_llinas, but please don't expect them to actually post anything.

**Quinn Burton** is an unwieldy gender problem haunting Durham, NC. They can be found on the baseball diamond with the Carolina Crawfish, and at assorted places online @holidayquinn(e)xpress.

**Quinn King** is a queer trans poet. Her work has appeared in the Lambda Literary Award-winning *2 Trans 2 Furious*, as well as in *Spillway*, *Pedestal Magazine*, *The Binnacle*, and others. She is originally from Seattle but now lives in Calgary, AB, with her wife, kid, and two rowdy cats. She misses the ocean.

**Rosie Accola** is a queer guido, poet, and writer living in Michigan. They graduated with their MFA in Creative Writing from Naropa University in 2022. Their first novel, *Supernormal Stimuli*, is out now with Bullshit Lit. You can say hi to them on Instagram @rosieaccola.

**Rowan Rivers** lives on a hill between an oak and a spruce on unceded Ohlone land. They also live with a dissociative disorder, their glorious partner, Daniel Rivers (also in *SCATC*), and their cats Nuala, Calcifer, and Wednesday.

**Sam Szabo** is a cartoonist and printmaker from the North Shore of Boston, currently based in Chicago, IL. Her debut graphic novel, *Enlightened Transsexual Comix*, was published by Silver Sprocket in 2023. Sam has seen Phish live 27 times.

**Sarah Esocoff** is an artist and journalist based in Brooklyn, NY. She is the creator of *Sounds Gay*, a documentary podcast about queer music culture. You can find her paintings, music, writing, etc. at sarahesocoff.com.

**Serena Hommes** is an actor, writer, and video creator. She is the star of *The Treadmill Switcher*, a queer comedy short film, and the upcoming sci-fi short film *Anastasis*. Originally from Missouri, she now lives under a giant cloud in the Pacific Northwest.

**Tuck Woodstock** is the host of the *Gender Reveal* podcast and the co-editor of *2 Trans 2 Furious*, which won a Lambda Literary Award btw. He lives in New York, just like those women from that show.

**véronique emma houxbois** (she/fae) is a trans woman pornographic romance cartoonist and leatherdyke based in Vancouver, Canada. Her autobio webcomic transcription lives at houxbois.org/transcription.